BEAUTY'S DADDY

A Beauty and the Beast Adult Fairy Tale

JANE HENRY

COPYRIGHT

Copyright 2017 by Jane Henry
All rights reserved.

No part of this book may be reproduced or distributed without written permission of the author, with the exception of small quotations for promotional purposes.

Please note this is a work of fiction. Any resemblance to real places or people is purely coincidental.

DEDICATION

I want to dedicate this book to those who helped me make it better! A huge thank you to my editor K.R. Nadelson, my proofers Jane B. and Alina F., to my dedicated betas Maisy and Kara, and to my ARC readers. Thank you so much for helping me bring my fairy tale to print!

SYNOPSIS

Once Upon a Time...

Sawyer:

They call me "The Beast" for a reason. Locked away in my cold, dark mansion overlooking the treacherous cliffs that haunt me, I want for nothing...except her. The moment she set foot in my lair, her fate was sealed. I will claim her, make her mine...

I'll be her daddy.

Annabelle:

He can buy anything he wants. He wants me.

He's a wealthy, domineering recluse; I'm dirt poor. He's accomplished and sophisticated; I'm a twenty-year-old virgin. But I can't say no. To get closer to him, I will sacrifice everything -- my freedom, my heart...my innocence. The attraction between us leaves me begging, and when he's done with me...

I'll be daddy's good little girl.

Beauty's Daddy is a full-length, standalone Daddy Dom/virgin novel, a retelling of Beauty and the Beast with mild BDSM themes and a guaranteed happily ever after.

Chapter One
ANNABELLE

Icy rain whipped my face and hands as I bolted down the length of Main Street. My mind a million other places, I turned the corner and crashed straight into the hugest, most arrogant, pissed-off man I'd ever laid eyes on.

"Jesus!" he roared, lifting the cup up to try to avoid spilling even more, but it was useless. "Watch where the hell you're going!" His deep voice startled me as he looked down from a lofty height, easily a foot taller than I was. So ashamed I could barely look at him, I was only vaguely aware that he looked familiar. He grasped his crushed coffee cup in one hand, a huge umbrella in the other, held so high over my head it did little to stop the downpour. Thick but well-kept stubble lined his sharp jaw, and black hair hung in savage, daring shocks across his forehead.

My mouth dropped open in horror. "I am so sorry," I said, looking around frantically but unfortunately there was nothing along the lines of stray rolls of paper towels or time turners that would help me make this predicament any better.

There was just me, a sodden, furious monster of a man, and a few bashful onlookers who went on about their business.

They were smart. He looked ready to kill.

I inhaled, prepared to offer my most sincere apology. He towered over me, easily a full head over my slight 5'1" frame. His hands flicked off excess coffee, while he growled, in a deep, husky, pissed-off voice that sounded more like a growl than polite conversation, "You ought to watch where you're going. For crying out loud, you could've burned yourself." He grunted, attempting to smooth out his clothing, but it was no use. He was a sodden mess. "Did you?"

I blinked. Did I what?

His eyes lifted to mine, brows knit with a furious glare, his lips thinned. "Burn yourself," he spat out.

I looked down at myself stupidly before responding. "No...I'm fine."

"Good," he muttered. "But for Christ's sake, watch where you're going." He turned to leave.

"Mister — whoever —" I sputtered. "I am so sorry I bumped into you like that. Please allow me to compensate you in some way, pay for your dry cleaning, or —"

He turned a scornful eye at me, lips turning down at the edges, his eyes raking me over from head to toe before he scoffed. "You couldn't afford it," he said, before he turned on his heel and left.

My stomach dropped, and then I realized that I was now officially late for work.

~

"*A*nnabelle!" So much for hoping that Linus, the overbearing owner of Diner on Main, wasn't in yet. "You're late?"

I frowned, turning away from him and hoping he'd get too busy to notice me again, when I heard a voice behind me.

"Do you have any idea who you just slammed into?" Lucy, the local librarian, was all about small town gossip, and knew every single person who ever set foot in any place at any time. She was even tinier than I was, with thick blonde hair pulled into a braid, sporting a short denim jumper. Perched upon a stool at the counter, her blue eyes blinked at me.

"No idea, Luce," I said, stepping out of my rain coat and shaking it off in the back room. "And I don't care. He's the biggest jerk I've ever —"

"*Annabelle!*" My stomach clenched and I barely stifled a groan.

"Good morning, Linus," I said as pleasantly as possible, taking my apron off a peg just behind the cash register and slipping it over my head as Linus came around the corner. Linus — a middle-aged dictator with wire-rimmed glasses atop his too-long nose, a thin moustache and a scant scattering of mud-colored hair across his head, frowned at me.

I fumbled to tie the apron in the back, when Lucy came over and did it for me, leaning in to whisper in my ear. "Don't mind him, honey," she said. "He's in a bit of a temper this morning."

When was Linus not in a bit of a temper?

"Do you know what time it is?" he grumbled, pointing up to the clock.

I can tell time, dumbass.

Releasing a shuddering breath, I nodded. "Yes, sir. 7:07. Looks like my lucky day?" But humor was lost on Linus.

"That'll come out of your pay," he grumbled, as he snatched a wad of napkins from the counter. "Go serve the table with the three kids over there."

I inhaled, shot Lucy a forced smile, and stepped over to the table where three moms with toddlers were having morning coffee. I took their orders, catching a small glass of orange juice before it spilled, and doing my best to put on a smile despite the fact that my head pounded from lack of sleep, my stomach growled in hunger, and I felt like bursting into tears.

I turned to go to the kitchen to place the order with Lucy following me.

"I didn't get to tell you who that was," she hissed in my ear. "It was —"

"Annabelle!" boomed a familiar voice.

Oh, for God's sake.

I closed my eyes, stifling another groan, as Lucy grabbed my hand and squeezed.

Her high-pitched voice piped up. "She's working, Gavin. Bug off!"

I bit the side of my cheek to keep from smiling. I adored Lucy.

Gavin, true to form, ignored her as he plunked down on one of the spindly chairs by the bar. "Cup of coffee, baby," he said. "You know how I like my breakfast." Gavin Montgomery, the local news reporter and small town heartbreaker, flicked his fingers across his cell phone, tipping his head to the side with a cocky grin. He tapped the phone, and a flash illuminated his straight white teeth. As always, he was dressed impeccably, in a tailor-made suit, blue button-down shirt and tie, his hair perfectly coiffed. He was like a small-town Superman in designer duds.

"Selfie of the day, Gavin?" I muttered. "And no, I don't know what your usual is."

Sliding his phone in his pocket, he smoothed out the nonexistent wrinkles from his suit. "Egg white omelette, lean ham, and fruit bowl, baby."

"Linus doesn't carry lean ham, Gavin," I said. "You know

what he carries. Standard breakfast sausage and bacon. And I'm not your baby."

Gavin frowned. "All those nitrates. Is he at least carrying free-range eggs yet? Or still in the dark ages?"

"Dark ages."

He shook his head and reached for my hand. His fingers were cold, his palm clammy, and I yanked my hand out of his.

"I'm working, Gavin," I chided. "Let me put in your or—"

But he was too fast. His hand snaked to my waist and pulled me to his side. "I know you're working, baby," he drawled. "But why don't you meet me for dinner tonight? I'll take you to a new little sushi restaurant over the bridge in town. We can drown our woes in sake and get to know one another a bit more."

"I don't like fish, and I despise sake," I lied. Though it was true I hated fish, I'd never tried sake in my life.

He frowned, his pretty blue eyes looking hurt. Damn him. "How could you not like fish?" he said, with a shrug. "It'll help you keep your girlish figure even after you bear children, you know."

My jaw dropped open. "Bear children? I'm only twenty years old, Gavin!"

He shrugged a shoulder, scoffing. "That's perfect. The younger you are when you bear them, the quicker you'll snap back into shape. Why not give it a whirl?"

I pulled away from him. "Putting in your order," I said, ignoring him as he continued to extrapolate on the benefits of women of childbearing years eating fish.

Lucy sidled up to me. "Can I spill his coffee on him?" The reminder of my early morning accident had me groaning out loud.

"God, don't remind me," I moaned.

"Remind you of what?" she asked, but just at then two things happened at once. My phone buzzed in my pocket at the very moment I heard a horrible screeching sound outside the diner, followed by shattering glass, wrenching metal, and shouts coming from outside. I pulled my phone out of my pocket. A text from my sister.

Mom is missing.

A feeling of dread pooling in the pit of my stomach, I tossed my notebook in my apron pocket, and ignoring shouts from Linus and pleas from Gavin, I ran outside with Lucy to see what had happened

My heart stuttered in my chest.

Just around the bend where I'd run into the huge jerk this morning were two cars twisted sickeningly, and one of them I knew all too well: my mom's old navy Buick, the one I'd carefully hidden the keys for the night before. The other? The most expensive-looking car I'd ever laid eyes on.

I raced to the scene of the accident as sirens screamed in the background and onlookers crowded around the cars.

"Mom!" Was she okay? God! She wasn't supposed to drive. She couldn't be trusted not to hurt herself, or anyone else. The dash was demolished, and windshield shattered. Oh, God. If she hurt herself…if she hurt anyone else…

"Annabelle!" My mom's wobbly voice came from the left, and when I turned, my eyes widened in disbelief. No way. No how.

God, *NO*.

My mom stood next to the man whose coffee I'd spilled this morning, his white shirt still drenched with the dark brown liquid. My mother rushed toward me, as his eyes narrowed on mine, his enormous arms crossing his chest.

"Mom, are you okay?" I asked, looking over her frail body. She was still wearing her pale blue pajamas, and a pair of slippers, her gray-streaked hair tied back in a messy ponytail, no glasses in sight. *God*. Where was Melody?

"I'm fine," my mom said, with a wave of her hand. "But

this one over here thinks it's fine to run stop lights. He ought to be put in jail!" She glared at the man, whose eyes narrowed even further. His jaw clenched as he glared right back at her, pulling his phone out of his pocket and putting it up to his ear. He pointed one angry finger at me, commanding me to stay right where I was.

There was no need. I wasn't going anywhere.

As police cars pulled up with flashing blue and red lights, I grimaced, and a stranger stepped up to me, an elderly woman with a raincoat pulled tight about her. "She's at fault, ma'am," she said. "I saw the whole thing."

"You hush your mouth!" my mom began.

I put a placating hand on her arm. In the early stages of dementia, my mom was in no position to be driving, let alone giving an accurate account of what happened, which was why I'd hidden the keys to begin with. My sister was supposed to be on duty.

"Mom, please be quiet," I whispered, trying my best to keep my cool, when the big beast of a man shut off his phone and stalked over to us, joined by two police officers and a paramedic crew.

His deep voice commanded the situation, as all eyes went to him. "The light turned green, and I began to drive," he said, "when this ancient piece of junk slammed right into my passenger side."

"How dare you call me an ancient piece —"

He held up a hand. "I'm talking about your *car*, not you. Please do not interrupt me. Fortunately, I was alone and it appears no one was truly hurt. The cars, on the other hand, are totaled." His eyes narrowed on me. "Am I to presume that you are the one responsible for this woman?" His gaze wandered over her pajamas and slippers.

I swallowed, embarrassed by my mother's display, horrified at the damage she'd caused, but furious at his dismissal of the one person I loved more than anyone in the entire world.

"Yes," I said, through clenched teeth. "This is my *mother.*" I glared back at him, defying him to insult my own flesh and blood. His eyes narrowed on me, but he said nothing.

"Annabelle," Officer Jones said gently. I went to school with this guy, and knew him well. With a sigh, I looked at him and nodded. "We've talked about this before, okay? Allowing your mother to drive like this, without supervision, is very dangerous."

"Matthew," I began. "I—" but it was too late. My mother heard all.

"How dare you talk about me as if I'm a child?" she said, her voice carrying over the crowd as my hand goes to her arm, attempting to calm her.

"Mom—"

"I am no older than your mother, Officer, and I am perfectly capable of driving. If *this* one over here hadn't been driving like such an idiot, we wouldn't have gotten into an accident!"

I sighed with practiced patience. "Mom, calm down. We need to get you examined," I said, hoping to distract her. I looked to Matthew. "Can we give a report at the hospital?" I asked him.

He nodded. "Of course, Annabelle. I think they both should be checked out. Mrs. Symphony, try to relax, and we'll bring you in to make sure you're okay." He turned to the big guy who was still glowering as if he were ready to breathe fire. "And you, let's get you looked over as well."

I turned my back to both of them, closing my eyes as the paramedics looked over Mom.

His car was worth more than my entire house. How would we ever get out of this?

Chapter Two

SAWYER

I punched numbers on my phone until I finally reached Alvin, my assistant.

"Where are you?" he questioned. "I've got the consultants from Senora Enterprises waiting, and I'm not sure how much longer I can hold them off with playful banter."

"Cancel the meeting," I said. "Tell them I was in a car accident, and I'm on my way to the hospital."

"Jesus, Sawyer, are you serious?" I scowled at the paramedic trying to wrap one of those stupid blood-pressure cuffs over my arm. Did I *look* like I was injured? All I needed was for my face to be plastered all over the local paper...again. The one day I decided to shrug off reclusivity and come into town for this god-awful meeting I needed to attend, and I end up with a coffee plastered suit and a totaled Aston Martin.

Fuck.

"No, I feel like playing a practical joke," I hissed into the phone, wanting to reach in and throttle him with my bare hands.

He sighed. "Are you okay?"

"Besides my car being totaled and my suit wrecked?" I twisted my neck, ignoring the pain when I moved, and my aching temples. "I'm fine."

"I'll be there within the hour," he said.

"Don't bother. Reschedule the meeting." I ended the call and slammed my phone into my pocket. The young paramedic, a boy with hair cut so short he looked like he was prepared to enlist in the army, looked up at me with wide eyes.

"Just need to get your pulse, Mister Gryffin," he said, putting two fingers on my wrist.

I merely stared, not deigning to dignify the aggravation with a response.

His eyebrows shot up, and he entered something into the tablet on his lap. "Your blood pressure is high, but all other vitals appear clear. You seem to be mostly unscathed, Mister Gryffin," he said. "But we should double-check signs of concussion at the hospital."

"Fine," I growled, stone facing him into silence as he waved a light in my eyes, and without thinking, I swatted his hand away. Good. Nothing like a growl or show of temper to get people to shut the fuck up.

We pulled into the parking lot of the hospital, as I allowed them to take me into the ER, noting the ambulance carrying the girl and her mother pulled in right next to us.

I still could not believe she'd allow her mother to drive unaccompanied. Her mother, clearly mentally unstable, was a menace to society.

As the doors to the hospital opened, they pushed me inside, followed by the girl and her mother. The girl wouldn't make eye contact with me. Who could blame her? But as I did my best to make her squirm under my penetrating glare, I looked her over. She was a bit odd, but... beautiful. I began to think of a way I could make this all very much worth my while.

~

The night was growing dark now. I waited impatiently for my paperwork so I could be released, when a tentative knock came at the door.

"Come in," I barked, expecting the third nurse to come in to take my blood pressure for the umpteenth time, but to my surprise, the small brunette who'd spilled coffee all over me stepped into the room. Her huge brown eyes were wide and fearful, which pleased me.

I liked people being afraid of me.

"What do you want?" I asked, my teeth clenching. I wanted to be home, not talking to the girl yet.

"I wanted to apologize," she began, her hands clasped in front of her. She still wore her diner uniform and her nametag.

Annabelle.

"You ought to apologize," I snapped. "First, for ruining a perfectly good suit and second, for allowing your mother to roam the streets unaccompanied. She could've hurt someone, or herself."

"I know," she began, her eyes pleading with me to understand.

Fuck understanding.

"But if you'd only listen to me. First, bumping into you this morning was an accident, and I already offered to pay —"

"If you were paying attention, you wouldn't have bumped into me."

Her eyes now flashed at me in anger. "I already apologized for that. Will you let me continue, or do you intend on interrupting me for the remainder of our conversation?"

I eyed her thoughtfully. She had spunk, this one. I was used to people cowering when I spoke to them, skirting away when I entered the room. Not this girl, however. And her formal trick of speech was oddly...attractive. I leaned against an examination table pushed up against the wall and crossed my arms.

"Go on, *Annabelle*," I stated. "You have one minute."

She started, and my eyes dipped to her name tag. She looked down and groaned, then took it off as she talked.

"My sister was supposed to be supervising my mother, who is not supposed to be driving, but she snuck the car keys and went out anyway."

"Why shouldn't she be driving?"

The bravado left her eyes, then, as she looked at me and her voice dropped. "She has early onset dementia. She forgets things, and frequently gets herself in trouble."

I refused to pity her. I despised pity.

"I see. And she is safe where you have her?" I asked.

She crossed her arms on her chest. "Excuse me, but that's none of your business."

Anger coursed through me. This girl had nerve. Did she not know who I was?

"None of my business?" I repeated, getting to my feet, enjoying how she shrank back when I towered above her. "It's none of my business that your mother plowed into my car, totaling it? She could have killed me, herself, or any other innocent who happened to be in her path. And that car is an Aston Martin, little girl."

Her eyes narrowed. "She did *not* hurt anyone," she said hotly. "She merely hurt your car, and for that I apologize, but certainly a man like you can file a claim? I mean, if you could afford a pompous, showy car like that, surely you can afford insurance?"

I raised a brow at her. "You call that an apology?" I asked, angry now that she had the nerve to come in my room and toss pathetic excuses at me. My palms itched to spank that sass right out of her, to teach her to watch her mouth.

Her gaze flitted away from me for a moment. "It *is* an apology," she insisted, as if she just realized the error of her ways.

"Is that right?" I growled, drawing closer to her, so close I could smell the faint citrusy scent that hung about her. "Then clearly you need a lesson in sincere apologies, and it would be my pleasure to teach it to you." And just like that, the air in the room changed. Desire coiled low in my belly, and the girl looked up at me, an innocent who'd made her way into my lair.

Her hand went to her throat, and she swallowed, her gaze never leaving mine, but when she spoke her voice was husky. "Oh?"

She was fucking aroused.

Shit.

I took a step closer to her. "*Oh.*" We were now mere steps apart, so close I could see the little bridge on her nose wrinkle when she shivered, and the pulse beneath the thin skin at her temples. "Lessons in humility," I said, not caring that I was living up to my reputation as a monster, a man bent on incurring the hatred of those around him with little concern for societal norms or expectations. "Lessons in safety," I said, stepping even closer to her. "Lessons in *obedience*."

She blinked. "I thought we were talking about my mother," she whispered.

I narrowed my eyes. "And I thought we were talking about apologies." I watched as her chest heaved up and down, and the pink-tipped edges of her fingers traced along the naked skin at her collarbone. Her shoulders were slight, but her body was all lush curves, from the swell of her breasts to the voluptuous rounded thighs. I enjoyed watching her fear, reveling in the knowledge that I was the one who'd brought this on.

I'd lived alone for a full decade, a bachelor and a recluse, bent on staying apart from others, and now here I was, the one day I ventured into town an absolute disaster. It seemed I'd go down in flames.

Annabelle stood with her back straight, her dark brown eyes trained on mine. "Then let's stay on the topic at hand, Mister..." her voice trailed off.

"Gryffin," I supplied, taking one step closer to her. "And yes, you may call me *Mister Gryffin.*" There would be no casual exchange between us. I would have the upper hand.

She swallowed. "Very well, Mister Gryffin. I wanted to ask how I can repay you."

I crossed my arms on my chest and fixed her with a stern glare. "Annabelle, are you aware that the car your mother destroyed was worth over $200,000?"

Her jaw dropped open. "Two hundred thousand dollars?" she gasped.

"Yes," I answered. "The suit alone cost three thousand." Custom-made, shipped directly from Italy. I owned half a dozen just like it, but she didn't need to know that.

She closed her eyes briefly. I could see it, then, her desperation, the hopelessness she wore like a second skin. If I were a good man, I'd have granted mercy. I'd have come up with a way for her to give what little she could, capitalize on my insurance payout and live happily ever after.

But I was not a good man.

I did not need the money. I needed *her* for a very specific purpose, but she'd learn about that on *my* terms.

"I'm a businessman, Annabelle. A man used to closing deals in his favor. Would you like to negotiate with me?"

I don't know what came over me. I have no idea where the thought came from, but one thing I knew for sure. I had come to town hoping to maintain obscurity, and her foibles threatened to drag me out into the light of day.

I would hurt her for that.

"Your mother is the one that owes me, not you," I explained, trying the sympathy tact so I could hedge my bets. "I could have her work for me to pay off her debt."

Her eyes widened. "My mother cannot work for you!" she protested, which was exactly what I hoped she would say.

"I — *I* could work for you, Mister Gryffin," she said, as if she were the one that had the thought, as if it hadn't been my intention from the very beginning.

"*You?*" I asked, attempting to appear disbelieving.

"Yes," she said, insistent now, emphatic. "I can work to pay off what we owe you."

I pretended to think it over, when instead what I really did was hide my glee from having lured her straight into my trap. "Very well, Annabelle," I said. "Why don't you come to my house tonight at eight o'clock. I'll take your cell phone number, and have my driver pick you up."

I jotted down the number she gave me and slipped it into my pocket.

"And Annabelle? Don't be late. If you are, I might have to give you your first lesson."

She blinked hard, but nodded with a smile. "I am never late, Mister Gryffin."

I smirked to myself. Really? We would see about that.

Chapter Three
ANNABELLE

Getting Mom situated at home proved easier than I anticipated, the events of the day wearing her out.

"I did not cause that accident," she insisted, and even though I had eyewitnesses and a big, glowering man who said otherwise, I merely placated her and urged her to go take a nap while I prepared dinner. She finally did, and I pulled out veggies and started chopping, as Melody joined me in the kitchen.

"Annabelle, this is crazy," she said, her voice low. Neither of us wanted to disturb Mom, and we definitely did not need her in on our conversation.

"What?" I said, pulling out a can of tomato sauce. I cracked the lid with the can opener and set it on the counter, chopping up onions to make a pasta sauce. I turned around to face her, wiping my hands on my apron. She sat at one of the three small chairs that hugged our tiny dining room table. My sister had recently dyed her hair with purple streaks, freaking mom out, but apparently her new boyfriend totally dug it. She twiddled one of the five silver rings on her fingers, and bit her lip.

"You did say Mister Gryffin?"

"Yes," I said, turning my back to her again.

"*The* Sawyer Gryffin?" The little hairs on my arms stood on end.

"I have no idea what you're talking about," I said, before I remembered vaguely that Lucy had said something this morning about the guy I'd spilled coffee on.

"That guy hasn't left his house in like a decade," she said. "In fact, he's not even *allowed* to as far as I knew. I thought he was on house arrest or something."

A cool sensation tickled the back of my neck. "What are you talking about?" I asked, my voice dropping as I tried to stay nonchalant, stirring the sauce on the stove.

My breath grew shorter, a horrible sense of foreboding overcoming me as I turned to look at her.

"He killed his fiancée, Annabelle. Years ago. They were never able to prove it, but he became a recluse, and yeah, he wasn't arrested, but that man is a murderer."

Murderer.

The words echoed in my mind's eye. I could picture him in front of me, the dark eyes beneath heavy brows, the chiseled jaw, his enormous stature, hands so large they could snap me in two with ease. He dwarfed the small hospital bed.

But did he have the eyes of a killer?

Was that something you could *see* on a person?

And if he really *was* a killer, why wasn't he in jail?

"Well, whatever, Melody," I said with false bravado. "He's not in jail or anything now, and maybe you're confusing him with someone else."

"Just be careful, Annabelle. Please," she implored. "Seriously, sis, Sawyer Gryffin is bad news and I'm not crazy about you going up to his house."

I closed my eyes, a headache forming at my temples. I rubbed my fingers over my forehead, trying to stave off the pain. Hoping to wash this whole damn day away.

I turned back to the stove and shrugged. A part of me was curious. Not only did I want to see where he lived, but I couldn't deny the fact that the man affected me. The way his deep voice scolded, his dark eyes never looking away. The expression on his face, harsh but...I couldn't put my finger on it. There was something about the man that attracted me. I swallowed.

"Mel, do you realize his car that Mom totaled cost over $200,000?"

I jumped as her hand slapped the table behind me. Turning around, I wasn't surprised to see her scowling. "What kind of dumbass buys a $200,000 car? Huh? And then expects someone who makes hardly anything to pay him back? Doesn't he have insurance that would cover it?"

"I'm sure he does, and I asked him that very question," I said. "But...well, I hate to admit it, but I spilled coffee all over his suit and ruined it." I swallowed, squinting one eye as I looked at her sheepishly. "And he says the suit alone cost three thousand dollars."

Mel's jaw dropped. "Did you, like, walk around all day trying to find ways to ruin Sawyer Gryffin's life?" Her eyes twinkled though.

I barked a laugh. "It seems like it, huh?" I turned back to the stove, and shook some salt into the sauce. I had to approach this topic carefully, as my younger sister's protective instincts were clearly on overdrive. I covered the sauce and cracked the lid a bit, allowing it to simmer, then came to sit beside her. The table was bare except for a small set of ceramic salt and pepper shakers I'd made in a summer art class years ago, back before my father died. I traced the edge of one, a clumsy, clunky blue piece my mom refused to get rid of. "You know, it isn't just about the money, Melody. Really." I turned the shaker in my hand. I remembered making it in a ceramics class we took at school once, how proud I was to bring it home, and how my dad had always said his food tasted better when seasoned with salt from this little shaker. "But I was afraid that if I didn't cooperate with a guy as wealthy and influential as Mister Gryffin, that if he began to pry, and found out how few assets we have…"

It was a gross understatement. We did not have any "assets." We lived in a tiny house, and on a shoestring budget. Melody made hardly anything sacking groceries at the local store in between classes at the community college, and I wouldn't take her money for bills anyway. My salary barely made ends meet, and Mom had medical expenses that ate away at my meager income. We made our food from scratch, shopped at thrift stores, shared the one car, and made do with as little as we could.

My voice dropped to a whisper. "What if he pried about Mom, Mel? What if he told someone she ought to be in a home or something? I think I can at least hear his plan out, see what he has to say, and maybe we can avoid owing him money for the rest of our lives. Maybe he'll let me off easy."

She frowned. "Listen, back in my freshman year I had to research local legends, and he was one of them. I honestly forgot all about him because he never comes around. I thought he moved or died or something, until you mentioned his name. Big guy, right? Like, huge?"

I snorted. "Enormous." My stomach dipped a bit as I remembered standing toe-to-toe with him.

"Yeah, so the Incredible Hulk had a famous fiancée, some rich chick from overseas whose dad owned a clothing company. They were engaged. Rich meets rich, they get richer, and everyone lives happily ever after, right?"

I shook my head, still laughing. "Right. Not exactly in my line of experience, but okay."

"And they had like this huge, epic fight, and people say that he pushed her off a cliff near his home."

I suddenly didn't find the story very funny, as I imagined those huge hands of his and those dark, angry eyes. I swallowed. "Oh?"

"Yeah. He claimed it was an accident, and with the kind of money that guy makes, you know he's got top-notch lawyers on his payroll. So to make a long story short, he was acquitted. But the townspeople never believed him. So he's been locked away up there in his ginormous mansion for like an eon. Word is that he has two servants who work for him, but they never talk to anyone about anything ever." She looked me square in the eye. "I seriously don't like the idea of you being anywhere near him."

I got to my feet then, and headed back to the stove, lifting the lid and stirring the sauce. "Hey, I don't like it either. But I highly doubt this guy is going to push me off a cliff or anything." Though I was trying to make light of the situation, I shivered. It was an eerie thought, and one I did not relish. "Anyway, like I said, I have good reason to go, Mel. I can't stand the thought of anyone taking advantage of Mom, or, God forbid," I turned to face her and dropped my voice. "Making her go to a home or something. You're going to *have* to stay here and watch her tonight while I meet with Mr. Gryffin, and then we'll have to make sure she's supervised. Got it?"

Melody shook her head. "I still don't like it."

At this point, my stomach was tied in knots at the thought of meeting Sawyer Gryffin, and it aggravated me. "I actually didn't ask you to like it," I said, meeting her gaze squarely. I was, after all, the big sister.

Her shoulders slumped, and she nodded with pursed lips. "Fine. Just be careful, dammit."

My phone buzzed, and I picked it up, nodding to her. "Yep. No long, romantic walks along cliffs. Check."

I frowned at the phone, not recognizing the number at first. *I'm sending a driver to pick you up at 8 o'clock on the nose. Do not keep him waiting. I'll be checking back.*

I swallowed, turning my back to Melody so she wouldn't see my hands shaking as I stirred the sauce.

I would not be late.

I stared at the pile of clothes on my bed and glanced at the time. What exactly did one *wear* when meeting a huge, filthy rich, supposed murderer for...what? Dinner? A bargaining arrangement? I had no idea what to expect from Sawyer Gryffin. I finally settled on a sensible outfit, a simple skirt and pink top with a pair of ballet flats, and ran a brush through my long, wavy brown hair, the one feature of mine I actually liked. It hung down nearly to my waist, though I never wore it like that, always braiding it or tucking it into a bun. I glanced quickly at the time, wondering if I had time to put the clothes away before I left. I hated leaving messes behind.

Damn. Two minutes to spare. *Two minutes?* Where had the time gone?

Do not keep him waiting. I could practically hear the man's deep, growly voice admonishing me to get my shit together and get downstairs. I quickly slapped some lip gloss on and ran a mascara brush through my lashes, when it dawned on me. Why was I rushing around like a madwoman to do what this guy told me? He wasn't my boss. I planned on meeting him to discuss ways to compensate him for damages. He was not going to *fire* me. And he could breathe fire all he wanted, but he was not in charge of me. Shaking my head, I put away my make-up in my bag, and grabbed some hangers. I was going to hang my clothes up, and damn him and his driver.

I paused, a little summer dress in one hand, a hanger in the other. "Well I'm not going to go running like I'm Cinderella and my clock strikes at midnight," I muttered to myself.

For some reason, the very thought of the growly Gryffin being Prince Charming made me laugh. I shook my head, and continued hanging clothes up in the closet.

My phone buzzed in my pocket, and I picked it up, feeling a strange surge of power as I glanced at the screen.

My driver has been waiting. Do you want to negate our arrangement this early, Annabelle?

Negate our arrangement? What the hell? I only wanted to knock him off his high horse a bit.

I shoved my phone in my bag, and left my room. Melody was waiting by the door, her arms crossed on her chest, shaking her head. I ignored her reminder that she didn't approve.

"Okay, I'm outta here. If I'm not back by tomorrow morning, call the police." Though I was totally joking, her eyes grew concerned and widened.

"Annabelle—"

"Oh my God, I'm joking," I said, giving her a peck on the cheek. "Be good." And with that, I left our tiny bedroom, and walked downstairs, my heart tripping in my chest. What did the night hold for me? Did he expect an answer to his bossy text? I huffed, opening the door, expecting to see some kinda Mercedes or something waiting for me. My jaw dropped when I saw a huge, gleaming black limousine waiting out front, with a well-dressed, stocky man leaning up against the door. His arms were crossed, and he bowed when saw me.

Was this the little town of Whitby? Or had I somehow transported to an alternate reality? It was bizarre, this elaborate limo out front with this driver waiting for me on my tiny street in front of my broken-down rental, while I stood there in a pair of scuffed ballet flats I'd bought at a thrift store for a job interview four years earlier. I swallowed, mustering all my bravado, and walked toward the limo driver. He had a bushy moustache and severe brows over stern brown eyes. "Mister Gryffin told me to be here at eight o'clock," he admonished. "I've been waiting."

Were all these guys like this? "Nice to meet you," I replied sarcastically, climbing into the luxurious, leather-scented interior. He shut the door, and opened his, sliding open the little screen between the back and front of the limo.

"Nice to meet you, too, Annabelle," he said. "But I do think it only fair warning to tell you that Mister Gryffin expects his instructions to be followed to the letter. He does not like to be left waiting. Please, for your own good, don't do it again." And without another word, he slammed the screen shut.

I frowned, but suspected that there'd be video cameras or something inside this ridiculous car, and even though I did not regret intentionally coming late, I didn't want to give Mister Gryffin, or whoever he was, any more fodder for his anger.

With a heavy sigh, I leaned back and observed my surroundings.

It was *amazing*. The floor was carpeted, the interior in complete black with silver accents. The seats were covered in a leather, and across from where I sat, a gleaming counter housed a small bar. He had a *bar* in his limo. Was he some sort of alcoholic? Who had an actual bar in their limo? A flat-screen TV flanked one door, but it was off, and no remote in sight. A pile of magazines stood up against one arm rest, but with titles like *Wall Street Today* and *The Enterprising Entrepreneur,* I took a pass. Not my thing. In moments, the nose of the car dipped upward and I tipped sideways. We were ascending a steep hill. I tried to look out the windows, but they were so heavily tinted it was hard to see much of anything, as night had fallen on Whitby.

I started when a voice came over a little speaker. "I'm sorry to disturb you," the driver said. "I prefer to keep my hands on the wheel and not use the screen when driving. May I get you anything, Miss Symphony?"

I shivered a little, unsettled being called by name by a complete stranger. I looked around the interior, unsure how to respond. Did I just speak into the air?

"Uh..." I began, looking around.

"Hit the button under your arm rest. The silver circle."

My cheeks hot, I pushed the button. "I am all set, thank you."

"Very well. We will arrive shortly."

I took the opportunity to press my face up against the window and cup my hand over my eyes, doing my best to look out the window. This helped, and I could now see a bit beyond the car. When I did, I gasped.

Waves crashed against enormous, craggy rocks, seemingly right on the other side of my window. God, how narrow was the road? The waves pounded with such ferocity I could almost hear the roar piercing the night air. In a panic, I pushed the button again.

"Yes? May I help you?"

"Oh my God, how close are we to the edge of the cliff?" I asked, my voice high-pitched and no longer even under pretense of having any decorum.

A responding chuckle did not alleviate my fears. "Far enough away, Miss. We're pulling up to the estate now."

I blinked. Lot of help *he* was. But my thoughts quickly shifted as I peered through the tinted window and saw a huge, black wrought-iron gate in front of us, as the driver's window lowered. He punched in a code, and the gates opened to the biggest, most majestic, terrifying home I'd ever laid eyes on.

Chapter Four

SAWYER

I expected her to defy me eventually, but not so soon.

The very first instruction I gave her, and she had the audacity to disobey? I paced the lush interior of my office, my hands behind my back, trying without success to control my temper. When the door creaked open, I turned on my heel, glaring, expecting the girl to be brought into my presence. However, Millie, the maid who'd served my family since I was a child, stood before me. She was an older woman with graying hair, with the appearance of an old-fashioned schoolmarm. She always wore a skirt and blouse in grays and blues with an apron, and she oversaw the cleaning of my house.

"Mister Gryffin, may I get you some tea? Coffee? A drink, sir?"

"No, thank you, Millie," I said, turning again abruptly to resume my pacing as I waited for the girl to arrive with Worthington.

"Sir, if I may offer you some advice," she began, coming in the room and shutting the door. I sighed, turning back to face her.

"No, you may not."

She blinked, folded her hands behind her back, and continued anyway. "You haven't entertained in years, sir, and honestly, if you are this angry with her before she's even set foot in the house —"

"Millie, you don't have the first clue what this meeting is about, or what I shall propose. Your job, need I remind you, is simply to do my bidding. Furthermore, I just told you I have no interest in advice."

She frowned, but bowed her head and turned to go. "Very well, sir," she said, as she opened the door. "I'm just reminding you that a bit of a gentle touch can sometimes go a lot further than your growls and blustering."

"Leave me!" The door closed with a bang.

Had I lost complete control of my staff, that she thought it fitting to scold me like a naughty child? My anger merely stoked, I walked to the sideboard and poured myself a drink, downing the fiery bourbon as a second knock came at the door. I inhaled, turning to face the door, and did my best to rein in my temper. "Come in."

When she walked in, I almost forgot I was angry. Gone was the drab uniform. Blacks and grays did not suit this woman. Her hair, no longer tucked into a matronly bun at the nape of her neck, hung down in loose, gleaming waves, a rich chocolate brown as dark as wet sand below my cliff. I wanted to wrap her hair around my hands, run my fingers through the silky strands, pull it until her mouth dropped open... and that *mouth*. How had I not seen the fullness of her rosy lips, now pressed in a firm line, attempting to pretend she was not afraid as she stood trembling before me? Wide brown eyes framed with long, black lashes, met mine across the room. She carried a small purse in one hand, which she clutched to her side as if her life depended on it.

"Sit down, Miss Symphony." It was no longer my temper I

fought to control but the arousal that coursed through me along with the whiskey — hot, liquid fire. I swallowed and nodded. The girl still stood by the door, and my anger flared to life again.

"I instructed you not to keep my driver waiting, and now you refuse to sit when bidden to do so?" I leaned against the sideboard and watched her through narrowed eyes.

Her eyes flitted about the room, taking in the large mahogany desk that flanked one wall, the stack of papers, the shelves filled to the brim with books, but still, she did not sit.

In my mind's eye, I crossed the room to her, grasped her slim wrist in my hand, sat on the arm of the couch, and dragged her across my knee. How I longed to lift that skirt of hers and paint her ass red for her defiance.

She'd learn I expected obedience.

"Excuse me?" she said, eyeing me curiously, her little chin lifted up as her eyes met mine. "I did not know you were *instructing* me. I thought you were inviting me. I'd rather stand, thank you."

And with that, my temper snapped.

I slammed my drink glass on the sideboard and stalked toward her. To her credit, she looked suitably afraid, her eyes widening, but she did not step away. I stalked until I was only inches from her. I grabbed her hand. Her bravado was a mere front. I tugged her over to the couch and pulled her to sitting before releasing her hand. "I do not have the time or patience for suggestions," I explained to her, mustering what little patience I possessed. "I told you when to be here. I told you to sit down. You've done neither. Now are you here to play games with me, or are you here to make amends?"

Her eyes closed briefly, and when she looked back at me, they were lit with fire. "I am here to make amends," she said, her voice dropping. "I apologize for being late."

I blinked, allowing a beat to pass before I spoke again.

She was in my clutches now. I had to play my cards well, but I also could use this situation to my advantage.

"I accept your apology," I said, wanting her to know that I needed more than that, that I needed control. But if I told her too much, if I pushed too hard, she would run. And I had to get her deeper in my snare, if I were to ensure my plan worked. I would test her, though. I would see how she reacted. "But although I accept your apology, I would like to explain something, Miss Symphony."

She raised a brow, folding her small hand on her knee, and though she tried to hide it, it trembled. "Oh?" she asked. Her voice was husky, her eyes lit with what I hoped was more than fear or curiosity.

"I am an exacting man," I said, allowing my voice to drop as I stared at her. We sat a little too close, our knees almost touching, as her eyes met mine. She swallowed. Her knuckles on her knee whitened.

She laughed, then, but it was forced. Her eyes still danced with fear. "Mister Gryffin, you don't need to spell that out. I have surmised at least that much with our interactions thus far."

Oh, she'd surmised *shit*.

"I have a small staff here, and the only ones I continue to employ are those who are willing to obey me." I could practically feel the increased tempo of her heartbeat as she stared at me unblinking. "I dismiss those who do not." I cocked my eyebrow at her. I wanted her questioning, wanted her curious. "I believe in authority and obedience, and as a successful businessman, I demand control."

She pulled her fingers through her hair, tucking it behind her ears, still pretending to be perfectly calm and collected. "I understand that, sir," she said.

Fuck.

Sir.

My cock thickened in my pants at the sound of *sir* on her lips.

I moved a bit closer to her on the couch. "I'm glad," I responded. She did not understand. But she would. "So I'd like to move on to a proposition. Instead of me taking you to court, or demanding you pay me for the damages against my person and property, I would like to make you an offer."

I watched her chest rise and fall with her labored breathing. "Mister Gryffin, does the offer of a drink still stand?"

I bit my cheek to keep myself from smiling. "Certainly," I said, rising and walking over to the sideboard. "What's your poison?"

"Do you have white wine?" I had chardonnay, pinot grigio, sauvignon blanc, viognier from all over the world. "Of course. Host's choice?" I asked, but I had already chosen. The question was a mere formality, as was her little nod. I poured her a glass of Montrachet chardonnay from France, the most expensive wine I owned. She held her glass and took a long pull, holding onto the stemware awkwardly, as if she were a child with a too-big cup. After a greedy sip, she removed her mouth, that beautiful lush mouth, and licked her lips.

"As I was saying," I continued, allowing my voice to deepen to get her attention. "A proposition."

Seemingly emboldened by her liquid courage, her shoulders straightened and her gaze met mine. "Yes?"

I was well versed in propositions, convincing my clients that what I had to offer was in their best interest. I had clients practically begging me to take their money.

And I did, over and over again.

But with her, I was proposing something far riskier, with a greater reward. "I need you to pretend to be my wife for a month."

Her lovely mouth dropped open, her eyes the picture of shock as she stared wordlessly at me. I needed to push this, explain my proposal, and convince her of the merit of what I asked before she wrote me off as a madman.

"It won't be difficult," I said. "I don't know how much you know of my life, Miss Symphony," I began, and she shifted on her seat, her eyes looking away from mine, guilt if ever I saw it. She knew enough. "But I've been a recluse for a full decade. And now *Le Point* magazine would like to do an article on the country's most wealthy businessmen. To deny the interview would be foolish," I said. "It is an opportunity to market myself and my brand, an opportunity I cannot pass up." There was more to it...so much more to it. But she did not need to know how I longed for this chance, to prove myself not a monster but a human. "I will require very little of you, and if you do as I ask, not only will your debt to me be forgiven, but I will pay you ten times your monthly salary."

Her fingers grasped her neck, clasping at imaginary pearls. "Ten times?" she whispered. The desperation in her voice almost undid me. I felt an unwelcome sympathy for this woman, in such desperate need of money and assistance. I'd researched her. She was damn near impoverished.

"Ten times. And your every need would be met. I would buy you a wardrobe, and anything else you need. But you will not be allowed to leave. I do not wish for you to speak to the reporters, but merely give the illusion of being a happy recluse like me. You will dine with me in my hall, and spend time with me, so the locals see I'm not a monster, and you will have the freedom to roam our grounds and my home." I paused. "*Mostly*. There are some areas that I will ask you stay away from so that I can have my own privacy."

Her gaze flitted over my shoulder, fixed on the world globe that stood in shadow on a shelf. It was outdated but one of my most prized possessions, not because of its worth or beauty but because my mother had purchased it for me.

"My mother..." she began. "I...I don't know if I can leave

her alone for that long," she began. "Is there any way I can merely visit you and pretend —?"

"No."

I hated not having what I wanted. Hated when what I desired was out of my reach. I would have this woman in my house if it killed me. I had to solve the issues that barred her from accepting my proposal.

"Do you have no one else in your home who could watch your mother for a month?" I knew her sister lived with her. I'd had her researched thoroughly this afternoon before following through on the plan I devised while in the hospital. But I didn't want to let on I knew where she lived, who she lived with, her birthday, and so much more. I know that she did not go to college, despite the fact that she graduated from high school as valedictorian three years prior. She'd stayed home to take care of her mother, and taken a job far beneath her just to make ends meet. I knew every penny of what she earned went back into providing for her mother and sister, and that she did very little for herself. Furthermore, I knew that her sister's last course ended this week, and that she'd be home now, if she did not take a job.

"My sister is finishing up her classes," she said, her chin at her hand as she echoed my thoughts. "She normally takes a few hours here and there tutoring over the summer, but if you are prepared to pay me ten times my salary, I could ask her to skip those summer jobs." Her voice trailed off, her gaze again on the globe. "I don't always trust her, though," she said. "She doesn't always pay attention."

"I could assign someone to assist her," I offered. What was I doing? I was getting in far too deep with this girl. Why her? Why did I have to choose her above all others? With my wealth and power, I could have just about anyone.

I did not want another woman.

I wanted *this* one.

"You mean...like a home health aide or something?" she asked. Her eyes softened as her gaze met mine, and in that moment, I'd have given her anything she'd asked, and I have it delivered to her on a silver platter.

"Precisely," I said.

She sighed, her eyes eager and excited. "Oh, that would be wonderful," she whispered.

"Consider it done," I said. "And I will arrange for you to have your job back when the month is up. I will pay your boss handsomely for allowing you to work with me."

"I see," she murmured. "So if I...accepted your proposal," she paused, faltering for a few seconds before she continued. "I would...pretend to be your wife." She swallowed, her eyes meeting mine once more. "What exactly would that entail?"

Though she sat stock still, I could feel it, I could see it, the rising of her chest, how her knees drew instinctively together as the tension between us grew. "You wouldn't have to share my bed, Miss Symphony, if that's what you're wondering."

"Goodness, no," she sputtered, but I continued as if she hadn't spoken at all, interrupting her.

"You will have a room of your own. I will have it leaked to the press that you do not speak to reporters and that you enjoy reclusivity with me. All you have to do is allow for a few discreet pictures to be taken, and when I allow it, you may be interviewed. But other than that, this is merely a front. The staff here will refer to you as Mrs. Gryffin, and the reporters shall do the same."

Never would I invite such an invasion of privacy into my life like this, but this chance...this one was different.

"I see," she repeated. "So all I have to do is live in the lap of luxury, pretend to be your wife for a month, and at the end, you'll pay me ten times my regular salary? That is all?"

I swirled my glass of whiskey and sipped, meeting her

eyes. "And obey me," I said huskily, allowing the words to settle over the room like nightfall.

I welcome the burning course of liquor down my throat, needing to be cleansed of my sins. I took another sip, and another, until only small squares of ice hit my lip, but I felt little more than a warm sensation curling in my gut.

"*Obey* you?" she asked, her brows furrowing. "As in, do what you ask of me?" She shrugged her shoulders. "Given you've asked so little, I expect that to be fairly innocuous, Mister Gryffin."

She was so wrong.

But I'd convinced her.

"Then do you agree?" I prodded. I would not detail my expectations of obedience. She was on the cusp of agreeing. It was time for me to close the deal.

She inhaled and exhaled once, twice, three times before she lifted the glass of wine to her lips and drank deeply, her eyes closed, until she'd finished her drink as well. She removed it from her lips. "I agree."

Chapter Five
ANNABELLE

I watched him from where I sat, as if in a trance. I would be a fool to pass up an opportunity to help my family like this. Not only would I no longer owe him anything, but I'd have nearly my entire year's salary at my disposal. What I could *do* with that money...

As I watched him pour himself a second drink, I wondered, though. What really went on inside the mind of Sawyer Gryffin?

What exactly did he *mean* when he said he expected me to obey him? He hadn't really given me any instructions yet. And a little part of me wondered still... did the virgin in me agree to this proposal because of the way he affected me? The very idea of being close to this man for a month not only had my pulse throbbing between my legs, but the way his voice chided me, the deep timbre of it riding over my body, caused a hum of desire to wind its way low in my belly.

As I contemplated, I watched him. His dark hair fell over his forehead as if he couldn't be bothered dealing with it. His eyes focused on something across the room but I did not know what. He swirled the glass in his hand, the ice tinkling as his jaw worked.

"I would prefer you not go back to your home to fetch your possessions. Rather, I will have whatever you need purchased and brought here."

I blinked. "Why can't I go back home?"

His eyes narrowed, then, and his jaw tightened. "I want you here with me," he said. "If you are to pretend to be my wife, and you're running back home to fetch things, it appears that you're not happy here."

Was that the real reason? I frowned, but did not question him. The truth was, I didn't even want to go back to my home. I liked the idea of one month off from the responsibility that had been weighing down on me for so long. I liked not having to worry about there being food in the fridge, and the bills being paid. For the first time, I was almost glad my mother likely wouldn't remember to ask for me or wonder where I'd gone.

"I'll tell you what," he said. "If it makes you feel any better, I will pay you a full half of your compensation up front. That way you can see I am a man of my word, and you can take care of whatever it is you need to beforehand. Call your sister, and make the arrangements."

Do this. Call her. Do that. Obey me.

Did he ever say please?

"Yes, I'd like to call my sister," I replied.

"Excellent. And while you do so, I'll have your first deposit wired directly to your account."

I gaped. That easy? He was going to pay me that much money as easily as someone might make a cup of coffee?

"May I step onto your balcony to speak to my sister?" I asked. His jaw tightened again, and his eyes flitted to the balcony before coming back to mine. What in the world?

"You may," he said. "But see to it you speak no longer than ten minutes. We have much to go over this evening."

I got to my feet, but something came over me then. It was odd, how this dark, commanding man affected me. I had never experienced anything like his enigmatic pull my entire life. I was not a submissive woman by any stretch of the imagination, but as he instructed me I could not help it. Automatically, I responded to his commands. "Yes, sir." His eyes warmed, and it felt nice. All of it. The approval in his gaze and the words *yes sir*.

I pulled my cell phone out of my pocket and stepped to the balcony, inhaling.

Melody was going to freaking flip.

"You *what?*" she hissed into the phone. "Annabelle, did he slip you something? Tell me you didn't eat or drink anything while you were there."

I snorted a laugh. "Um, Mel, he didn't slip me anything. I'm perfectly sane. Honestly, you would turn down this incredible offer?"

"That much money to live in the lair of Satan?" she asked. "Are you kidding me? You couldn't pay me enough."

I laughed harder. "Oh for God's sake, Mel, he isn't *Satan*. In fact, there's something about him I almost like."

"You don't even know him!"

"Nor do I have to. He's already paid half the money up front. I can transfer you what you need already. He says I don't even have to stay near him, but will have my own room with my own clothes and everything. It's just a month, honey, and I'll have nearly my entire year's salary." I had to do this. We had no car. Melody's book fees would need to be paid soon, as did our electric. And I knew for a fact all we had in the house for food was a loaf of bread, a jar of peanut butter, and leftovers from the night before. "Honestly, Melody, something tells me he's not going to hurt me. Let me do this for us." Though I pleaded with her, I'd already agreed. I was not going back on this now.

"He's sending someone here to help with Mom?" she asked in a small voice. Despite her vehement protests, I knew she wanted this as much as I did. It was hard caring for our mother, and the idea of a professional coming to help was every bit as enticing as the money he offered.

"*Yes.*"

"And you said he's already given you money?"

"It's already in my account."

She sighed. "Be careful, Annabelle. Please. If what they say about him is true..."

"I don't think it is, Mel," I whispered, eyeing Sawyer through the glass door that separated the balcony from his study. He stood, his arms folded across his chest, eyes focused on the clock on his mantle. "And I have to go. He said I only had ten minutes, and I'm past that now." Good. I wanted him to know that he wasn't in complete control, but if I were honest...if I were really honest...I wanted to know. What did he *mean* about obeying him?

What would happen if I didn't?

"Ten minutes! He's timing you? I don't know, Annabelle, I—"

"It's going to work out. Love you. Bye." And with that, I clicked the phone off, and shoved it in my pocket. Then with trembling hands, I pushed open the balcony door, took a deep, enervating breath, and went inside.

"I spoke with my sister," I began, but his harsh voice cut me off.

"You're late."

I glanced at the clock. "Am I?"

"I gave you ten minutes. You took twenty. This is not how we will begin things, Miss Symphony."

Though I'd agree to play the part, I needed to see what he was really all about.

"Oh? Did I? I didn't know you were watching the clock, Mister Gryffin. I am sorry I was late." But I wasn't. Not really. I wanted to stoke the fire within him, see his eyes flame. I needed to know *what he would do*.

"Come here, please," he said, his hands anchored on his hips.

My stomach flipped. Had I taken things too far?

But I obeyed. Shuffling over to him, my heart thundering in my chest, I could feel my panties dampening between my legs. I had never experienced anything like this in my life, desire stoked with fear. Something about the way he commanded made my nipples pebble, a fine sheen of perspiration dotting my forehead as I dragged my feet over to him. When I stood in front of him, I suddenly realized that he was far, far bigger than I'd thought. Just a foot away from me, I took in all of Sawyer Gryffin. He was dressed in black slacks and a white dress shirt, the collar unbuttoned, revealing a stark white vee of a t-shirt. The breadth of his shoulders dwarfed me, the thick muscles of his neck barely hidden beneath the fabric of his shirt. His chest loomed in front of me, his enormous hands placed on his hips, his fingers alone four times the size of mine. Standing in front of him, I felt tiny, the top of my head barely above the middle of his chest. I couldn't breathe. I forgot how to even think, as my gaze traveled the length of his body and upward, craning my neck, feeling the pull along my spine as I lifted my gaze to his.

To my surprise, his lifted his hand and cupped my chin,

the warmth of his touch making me quiver a bit. I swallowed. He spoke softly, as we stood so close, his voice as deep as a chasm, raspy. His question shocked me. "Did you have a father, Annabelle? Did you know him?"

I swallowed. "Yes, sir, I did, but he died when I was a young girl."

One nod. Acceptance and sympathy in his gaze, but sternness. "Did your daddy ever spank you?" If he hadn't been holding my chin, my jaw would have dropped open.

Oh my God.

Flames galloped across my chest and I couldn't breathe. I'd played with fire, and now I was about to be burned.

"No," I whispered, and then, "I was a good girl."

His eyes wrinkled at the edges as he smiled, but something lurked behind that grin, something wicked. "That's right," he said. "Good girls don't deserve spankings. Do they?"

My breath came in rapid gasps. "No, sir," I managed. "They don't."

He still held my chin in his hand. "But do little girls who don't do what they're supposed to deserve to be spanked?"

He was asking me?

What if I said no?

But...I couldn't. He made me feel things I'd never felt before.

"I...I don't know," I whispered, not wanting to tell him no, but too weak to tell him yes.

His eyes narrowed, darkening, his grip still firm on my chin. I could not look away.

"I believe naughty little girls who disobey should face consequences," he said, leaning forward and whispering in my ear, his breath moving little wisps of hair on my neck, goosebumps raising along my neck and arms. "Maybe Daddy needs to spank you, to teach you to mind."

Oh *God*. I closed my eyes, growing dizzy at his words, so aroused I could come just like this, just from his whispered words in my ear. Like a moth to flame, I could not turn away, but my pulse was beating a tempo so intense I could not reply. It was then that he released my chin, and pulled away from me.

"Lean over my desk, please," he instructed, waving a finger toward the desk that stood several paces behind us. In a trance, I obeyed, the shining desk pushed up against my belly, my hands splayed out in front of me. "There's one thing you need to know, little girl. While you're here, you'll do what Daddy says."

Oh *fuck*.

What had I gotten myself into?

With his huge hand at my waist, I shook like a leaf, my hands grasping the edge of the desk, and before I knew what was happening, his huge palm cracked against my bottom. "Ten minutes late? Ten spanks. The correct response is, *Yes, Daddy*."

I was going to fly out of my skin. Moisture gathered between my legs, the scent of my own arousal permeating my senses. I swallowed, licking my parched lips, and I whispered with my eyes closed, "Yes, Daddy."

Oh my God. It was so wrong but utterly delicious to call him Daddy.

I gasped as another swat landed, then another. It hurt like hell, his huge hand on my thinly-clad backside, but it wasn't unbearable.

Shit.

I liked it.

And then he was done. I was still fully clothed, and one more touch, one more whispered word, and I was going to come, right here, pushed up against the desk of a man who could have been a murderer, this beast of a man who demanded obedience. Fully clothed, and I was more turned on than I'd ever been in my life.

I gripped the edges of the desk as if they would somehow anchor me. I could not understand how his bossy, domineering ways turned me on. Wasn't attraction built on intellect, good looks, humor...or something? What was this animalistic attraction I had to this man? It made no sense.

Did it have to?

"Come here," he said. I could feel him standing behind me, and when I turned he stood, arms across his chest, eyeing me curiously. Did he wonder how I would react? If I would call the police, or my sister, or somehow freak because he'd just...*spanked* me?

I didn't know how to respond. We were already so far beyond what was normal or natural, that I didn't really know what to do with myself.

He cocked a brow, and his lips turned down at the edges. "Annabelle?" he said, his voice lowering, chiding. "I said come here. So soon after being punished you'd disobey me?"

When I was within a foot of him, he uncrossed his arms and reached for my chin, once more tipping my gaze to meet his, the dark of his eyes burrowing right through me as he stared. "Are you going to be sure you obey me?" he rasped. "You do realize that was only a warning, don't you?"

A low pulse in my belly responded before I did, my mouth dry. There was something in his eyes...no, it would not do to be getting soft for this big bear of a man.

Something told me, though, this man could not have *murdered* anyone. Anger, yes, that much I could see. He liked being obeyed and had little patience. But impatience did not make him a cold-blooded killer.

I nodded dumbly, not knowing what to say. My ass still stung from the heavy fall of his hand, but he'd only given me ten smacks. What would more be like?

Did I really want to find out?

"No," I said, shaking my head.

He gazed at me thoughtfully, as if deciding something, then he pulled me to him briefly, his arms around me comforting, sweet, chaste, and all too soon he let me go.

"I will see you to your room."

Chapter Six
SAWYER

It was much harder to restrain myself than I thought it would be. I'd fantasized about pulling her over my knee, draping her across my lap and smacking that cute backside of hers until she begged me for mercy. There was something about her pert little nose, the defiant, vibrant eyes, and her boldness that made me want to teach her who her daddy was.

I was a sick son of a bitch.

But I wondered if a part of her needed to know I meant what I said. Did she test me? She'd kept an eye on the clock and shown no surprise when I told her she was late. The only surprise came when I bent her over the desk.

I had no regrets.

I did not have her here so that I could take advantage of her. No. I'd pay her handsomely for playing the part of my wife, getting me off the hook with the media. For now, we'd play the part, and I was happy to pay her to do so.

I shoved open the door of the office, and gestured for her to walk through, as if we were just two old friends and I hadn't just pushed her up against my desk and spanked her ass.

My staff was waiting in the corridor. A part of me wondered if they'd heard anything. She had not cried out when I spanked her, and they knew to keep their mouths shut. After all, this was my house.

"Annabelle will be staying with us for a while," I said. "As far as all of you know, she is my wife. She has been for some years, but we keep our relationship under wraps. No one is allowed to answer questions posed by media. For your own purposes, we were married overseas in a small chapel. Should account for no record." I would get in touch with my contact who would make sure to have the proper paperwork on file if need be.

"She will be staying in the gable room in the east wing." I turned to Annabelle and fixed her with a stern look. "You are not to go in the west wing at all. That is where I have my private office, and even my staff does not step foot in my personal area. Do you understand me?"

She frowned, and her pretty eyes flashed at me, but she did not respond. Her gaze traveled to the huge marble stairs where the stairway split, one to the left and one to the right. The door that led to the west wing was locked, and even my staff did not have access.

"Fine," she huffed. I barely tempered a growl. Perhaps I hadn't spanked her hard enough. She'd learn to respond more politely.

"Would you like me to see her to her room, sir?" Millie asked.

"No, thank you," I said, walking up to Annabelle and taking her by the elbow. "Seems our guest is fairly curious, and I'd much prefer to show her to her room and lay down the ground rules myself." She tried to yank her arm away from me, but I held fast.

"Allow me," I said with mock politeness. I turned to Millie, whose wide eyes watched my interaction with Annabelle in wonder. "I would like you to order Miss Symphony whatever it is she needs. This evening, she will need something to sleep in, and whatever toiletries she is accustomed to using. Anything she wants, she gets." Wide eyes and silence followed my pronouncement, as I continued marching her up the stairs.

"You can let me go," Annabelle hissed at me. "I'm not going to run away like a scared little kitten or something."

Scared little kitten.

The lady doth protest too much.

"I can let you go," I said, "But I'd rather not. I much prefer having you by my side like this."

"Will you simply manhandle me when you don't get your way?" she asked from between clenched teeth.

"If you give me reason."

"That was not part of our agreement."

"Excuse me," I said, tightening my grip. "Obedience *was.*"

We walked in silence up the large marble stairs. She tried to pretend like she wasn't staring at my home as if we were in a museum. When I caught her looking at the marble stairs, detailed chandeliers hanging from the ceilings, and elaborate paintings on the walls, she'd look away, but when she thought I wasn't looking, she'd gape again. The ornateness of the place almost embarrassed me. I had not been the one to choose the furnishings, and couldn't be bothered with changing it all now. This was not a mansion or palace but my prison. Who cared what it looked like?

"This is a large home for only one person," was all she said.

I merely grunted in response.

"Do you...ever want to move?" she asked. "To a smaller

home, perhaps? Something with a bit more of an intimate setting?"

I did not respond at first, because they were details I didn't share freely. The townspeople were under the mistaken impression I was bound here by law. I was not. I chose to stay here, in this home of mine where ghosts haunted me even in my waking hours. Still, her incessant chattering aggravated me.

"A man of your stature could get a little—"

"Be quiet, Annabelle." She halted mid-sentence, and I felt guilty for being curt to her. She was only a pawn, after all. Only an innocent bystander. Irritated with myself, I could not prevent my temper from rising, and before I could stop myself the words tumbled angrily from my mouth. "You would know about smaller homes, wouldn't you? You practically live in a hovel."

With that, she yanked her arm away from my hand. I half-expected her to snap at me, but she said nothing, silently fuming as we finally reached the top of the staircase.

I'm sorry. The words were on the tip of my tongue, but I could not speak them. Her anger stoked mine, and I grunted at her to follow me.

"This way," I said, my words a barely understandable half-growl. I pointed in the general direction of the west wing. "You'll notice this stairway parts in two, and the one across from us leads to the west wing. You are *not,* under any circumstances, to trespass in that section of the house. The rest of my home is yours to roam at your leisure, but you are not to set foot in that area. Do you understand me?"

I groaned inwardly as her eyes lit with excitement and curiosity, peering at the forbidden doorway. "You've already said that." I wanted to shake her. I wanted to draw her across my knee and bare her, *really* spank her, punish her for her insolence.

But I had to control my temper.

" 'Oh' does not indicate that you've understood and plan on obeying me."

"Fine," she said. "I won't go to your precious west wing. Now will you show me to my room?" she spat out.

The *brat*.

I would not allow her to anger me further. I would not be baited.

"You will watch your tone of voice with me, young lady," I warned, narrowing my eyes on her as I continued to walk toward her. She squealed as I nabbed her hand and pulled her closer to me. "You don't want to push me, Annabelle."

Her chest heaved, her eyes furious, but I ignored her temper as I led her to the doorway to her room, but when I opened the door, her indignation melted away. Instead, her eyes widened in wonder, her lips parted, and she looked around like a child who'd just entered a candy shop.

"This is my room?" she whispered.

"Yes," I said, trying to hide the fact that her amazement pleased me.

It was the largest, most well-furnished guest room in my home, and I'd had my staff freshen it up before her arrival. A large, four-poster bed sat in the center of the room, filmy white drapes swirled across the posts. A thick white quilt adorned the king-sized bed, dainty hand-stitched red flowers adorning the edges. Half a dozen fluffy pillows sat at the head of the bed, and a folded pale blue throw blanket lay across the foot. Large bay windows lined the wall opposite the doorway, oval-shaped and adorned with intricate drapes. There was a desk with a chair, and a laptop, pens, and notebooks for her use. A pillow-topped bench lined one window, and in my mind's eye, I fancied her curled up there, a book in her lap, gazing out the window that overlooked the flower garden below. A heavy wardrobe sat in one corner, empty and ready to be filled, a large walk-in closet to the right, and there was a doorway to her bathroom between the closet and wardrobe. The bathroom had been cleaned until it gleamed, thick Egyptian cotton towels waiting to be used. Her clothing, though, would still have to be acquired.

"Tomorrow morning, you will meet me for breakfast at eight o'clock," I said. "We will meet with a fashion consultant who will help you pick out a wardrobe suitable for your stay here. And if you'd like, I can arrange for a...hair stylist...or, whatever it is you girls need to come help do your hair."

I expected her to be excited. I didn't know the first thing about girl things, and had only been trying to help, but instead, she frowned, her eyes shuttering. She didn't have a lot of money. Wouldn't she appreciate my generosity?

"I think I'm all set," she said. "If you insist on me wearing fancy clothes as part of our arrangement, I'll do that. But I don't like breakfast."

What an ungrateful little brat.

"I didn't *ask* if you liked breakfast," I said, my voice rising. "I told you to meet me for breakfast at eight o'clock. You *will* join me for breakfast, or you will answer for it." I stormed to her door and opened it. "I will have the consultant come to meet with you. You may pick as little or as much as you'd like, and you're welcome to take home everything that belongs to you when the month is up." I looked over my shoulder, giving her one final, parting glare. "I will see you tomorrow at eight."

"Fine!"

"Fine!" I shouted back, slamming the door behind me so hard the echo reverberated through the entire floor.

I wanted to *hurt* her, to punish her. Instead, I stormed away, hoping she felt badly for being so rude and inciting my anger. She'd show up for breakfast, or I'd teach her to mind.

Chapter Seven
ANNABELLE

I woke the next morning to the chirping of birds outside my window. I did not move at first, my eyes still closed, as I wondered if what had transpired the night before had all been an eerie dream. But when I opened my eyes, I could see filmy white curtains around the wooden posts of my bed, and my heart started to flutter wildly in my chest. Sitting up, I looked around, clutching the blankets to my chest as if I expected him to be lurking in the shadows. He was not there, of course. He might have been bossy and arrogant and even downright scary at times, but I didn't get the stalker vibe off him. I never would have signed on to do this if I had.

Or would I?

Pushing all niggling thoughts of how stupid I'd been out of my head, I lay down on the bed and tried to clear my mind. I would enjoy living in the lap of luxury. From where I lay, I could see a huge, oval-shaped tub, and a fancy pedestal sink. I longed to take a bubble bath in the enormous tub, to sink under the poofy foam and submerge myself in the fragrant water. The night before, I'd been far too tired to do much more than quickly wash up before slipping into the soft cotton pajama shorts and tops that waited for me on the dresser.

It was almost unsettling how perfect the clothes were for me — white with little pink dots, edged in lace, and super comfortable. They fit me to a T. Four more pairs of PJs similar to this one lay neatly folded in the top drawer.

Today I would pick out my wardrobe, supposedly.

I frowned, pulling the blanket up higher on my chin, though it wasn't exactly chilly in the room. I thought of our conversation the night before, as he told me I could pick out whatever I'd like to wear. Was I simply being stubborn? For the past eight years, ever since my mother had begun to show symptoms of mental illness, with my father no longer in the picture, my sister and I fended for ourselves. We could hardly make rent and utilities, so we'd relied on thrift store purchases and hand-me-downs from friends to supply our needs. Melody was a master at finding just the right clothing on mark-down day, and we both had what we needed. The mere thought of a stylist and new wardrobe boggled my mind. I could not imagine such luxury. Why had I resisted so vehemently?

I remembered the way he'd looked, his dark eyes furrowed beneath heavy brows, his stubbled chin jutting out as he mocked my home and poverty.

What an asshole.

My phone buzzed on the bedside table, and I glanced at the screen. Melody.

Hey. How are you doing? Mom's good here. I got a call that someone was coming to check on her this afternoon. I'll let you know how it goes.

I went to reply to the text, when the time in the upper right-hand corner of the screen arrested my attention. With a gasp, I dropped my phone, tossed the blankets aside, and leapt to my feet.

7:48.

I had twelve minutes to be at breakfast, or...or I didn't know what would happen. Though part of me flirted with the idea of being late, of showing this...*beast* that I was not going to be cowed by him, a small part of me wanted this to work. And I'd already played the testing card now, twice. I'd agreed to do what he told me. He was going to pay me handsomely in return. So when it came down to it, I really had nothing to lose and so much to gain. There would be a time to test his mettle, to show him I was no naturally submissive person who would do his bidding. However, the very first day at breakfast was not one of those times.

I opened the dresser drawers, astonished as they slid so easily along the tracks. My dresser at home was cheap particle board and the drawers needed to be yanked with every bit of my strength just to budge. This was heavy, quality furniture, solid wood, and I took only a second to draw my finger along the edge of the grain, in circles, while inhaling the smell of lemon furniture polish. This dresser alone would likely pay one month's rent.

What would it be like to know such luxury?

I didn't allow myself to dwell, as I needed to move. So much for showering before breakfast. The first drawer held a small handful of thankfully modest but pretty panties, white lace in a becoming bikini style, again in my size. Next to that were several other undergarments, a few white laced bras and folded socks. I flushed as my finger edged the pretty satin of the bra.

Had he picked these out?

I shut that drawer and opened the one below it. I hadn't packed, and hoped there was more waiting for me than pajamas and underwear.

In the second drawer, I found what I was looking for: three simple but elegant summer dresses, one a sky-blue with white accents, white piping around the edges, lightweight and casual. Another was a pretty sage green number with spaghetti straps, and a third a floral pattern of pinks, reds, and white, with an empire waist that would hit just above my knee. Swallowing hard, I shut that drawer and opened the third. A few pairs of jeans lay nestled to one side, some dark-colored and some light, straight legged and bootcut. To the right of those lay a few tops, but I shut the drawer quickly. I did not have time to peruse my "pre-wardrobe" before the fitting, as the clock was ticking. I grabbed my undergarments and the sage green dress, pulled my pajamas off, hurled them in the direction of the bed, and dressed in the sky-blue dress before I ran to the bathroom and tidied up.

I glanced at my still-bare feet. Had he thought of those, too? I skipped out of the bathroom and eyed my worn, plain black flats. They'd look dilapidated and outdated paired with the new dress. Cautiously, I opened the door to my closet, and my jaw dropped open. I could have easily fit my bedroom and Melody's in my closet alone. The shelves were bare but for half a dozen shoes. I quickly chose a pair of white leather sandals, and slipped them on, not even having enough time to look at the others.

The back of the closet door was a full-length mirror. I appraised myself with a critical eye. The dress fit well as did the shoes, and though my hair looked tidy, my face was barren of make-up. Inhaling deeply, I straightened my shoulders, put everything away, and raced to get my phone.

7:59. No time for make-up.

"Shit," I swore under my breath, as I ran to the door and yanked it open to reveal a vacant hallway. I knew I had to go down the large staircase to get to the dining hall, and hoped I'd find my way when I reached the bottom. Quickly heading down the stairs, my footsteps silent on the thickly carpeted steps, I made it to the first floor in record time. Once there, I looked around frantically. Where were all the servants that always seemed to be hanging around here? Muttering under my breath, I followed the sound of clinking glass and voices to my right. To the left, I saw the door to his study, the one where we'd made our agreement and he'd…I swallowed, smoothing down the skirt of my dress as I remembered leaning over his desk. I could still feel the sting of his palm.

To the right, thank God, I could see from the doorway a large dining table, and a wooden buffet table laden with dishes and silverware. I raced to the doorway and when I got to the entrance, I slowed down, pretending I hadn't been running around like a lunatic and I hadn't just woken twelve minutes ago.

When I entered the room, the voices halted.

"Miss Symphony."

I turned in the direction of his voice, keeping myself cool, calm, and collected. I nodded to Sawyer Gryffin, who sat at the table with a newspaper and a steaming mug of coffee.

"Good morning," I said, barely catching myself before I tacked *Sir* at the end.

No, I would not call the man sir.

I inhaled, and walked to the table, as he lifted the large, steaming cup of coffee to his lips, looking pointedly at his wrist as he did so. Was I a minute late? Would he bend me over *this* table, just as he'd bent me over his desk? He took a leisurely sip, then placed the cup down in front of his plate. "Thank you for being punctual, Miss Symphony."

Phew.

"Call me Annabelle," I said, with as much nonchalance as I could, so as not to betray my shaking hands and pounding heartbeat.

"Very well, Annabelle," he returned, and it was then that

he dropped the pretense of civility, his lips curling into a wicked grin as his eyes met mine. "I believe we've already discussed what you may call me."

I halted, my hand halfway to the chair in front of me. I would *not* give him the satisfaction of besting me and assumed he'd attempt to hide his kinky, deviant side from whatever staff lingered about.

"Have we, Mister Gryffin? I may call you Sawyer, then?"

His eyes narrowed but he smiled nonetheless. "No, sweetheart. I'd much prefer Daddy."

Despite his narrowed gaze, despite the fact that he'd pushed my comfort zone so far it had split wide open, my pulse accelerated at his words.

Daddy.

It was so wrong it was hot. Taboo.

Sinful.

Delicious.

"But I'll only allow you to say that when we're alone, if you prefer."

"Right," I stammered, not meeting his eyes and studiously ignoring his low chuckle as I grabbed the top of one of the heavy chairs and drew it out.

"Go get yourself something to eat, first," he ordered. I looked up at him. He held half a bagel in one hand while with the other, he smeared cream cheese across the lightly browned surface. His brows raised and he gestured behind him. "We weren't sure what you liked to eat, so we had a little bit of everything put out. For future reference, it would be good to know what you like."

I walked toward the buffet behind the dining table, which necessitated having to walk past him, my eyes widening at the enormous display. I'd never been to a breakfast buffet, but this looked like one that I could enjoy.

"You don't know what I like for breakfast?" I tossed over

my shoulder, lifting a heavy ivory plate from the end of the table that was still warm. "Seems you know everything else about me."

"Don't be smart with me," he said, his tone tight. Not wanting him to see me gripping my plate harder, I kept my back to him.

I hadn't meant to be rude. Well, not *that* rude. It appeared my sarcasm did not scan under his radar. I did not dwell long on this, though, as my widened eyes took in the large array of food in front of me.

A fancy glass cut bowl on a pedestal housed a variety of cut fruit and berries, strawberries ripe to the core, plump blueberries, and thin slices of red-tinged peaches. My mouth watered at the aromas that wafted in my direction, and I swallowed, scooping a generous portion of fruit salad on one corner of my plate. Next, an array of yogurts sat nestled on ice, and to the left of that, lay steaming trays of spinach quiche, crispy strips of bacon, and thick-cut hash browns fried with onions. To the left of the hot foods were oatmeal and baked goods, mini pastries with little dollops of cream cheese and lemon filling, a platter of bagels, and two pitchers, filled with what looked like freshly-squeezed orange and grapefruit juice.

"Is anyone else coming?" I asked. Why so much food for little old me? And I hated eating in front of people.

"No." I waited for him to offer more, but he did not. My hand shaking, I served myself a wedge of the spinach quiche and placed it next to my fruit salad, then chose one of the delicious-looking pastries before I turned to the table.

"No oatmeal today?" he asked, quirking a brow at me. I bit my lip to keep my jaw from dropping.

I ate oatmeal for breakfast every single day before I left for the diner.

He knew. And he was attempting to set me off kilter.

"No, thank you," I said, shaking out the folded napkin that lay on the tablecloth before smoothing it onto my lap. "As you likely know," I said, meeting his gaze now across the table, "I eat oatmeal every day, because it's inexpensive and easy to eat before work. I'm never treated to food like this, so it's a rare privilege."

He only met my gaze but did not respond, tearing a piece of his bagel with his hands. He chewed it methodically as he watched me. I hated that he watched me, but I was starving. I cleared my throat and finally looked down at my plate. He unnerved me, this man, and I didn't like feeling so flustered. Focusing on my food, I nabbed a piece of strawberry with my fork and popped it in my mouth. It was sweet and tart, and juicy. I followed that with a bite of the rich, flaky quiche. My stomach growled approvingly. I hadn't eaten a breakfast like this in years, maybe not ever.

"You tell me whatever you'd like prepared for you, and I'll see it is done," he said.

I smiled. "Aren't you afraid of spoiling me?"

The smile faded from his eyes, and he sobered, his lips turning down, but then he quickly recovered. "No, Annabelle. I am not worried about spoiling you." He paused and his eyes grew heated. "I thought I demonstrated last night that I'm quite capable of handling spoiled little girls."

My face heated. I suddenly wished I had a glass of juice next to my place. Honest to *God!*

I chose not to respond, focusing on my food instead.

"A question for you," he asked. He picked up his cell phone, hit the power, and when he lifted it, I could see a news clip on the phone in front of me. I almost dropped my fork.

"Do you know this man?"

I swallowed the food I was chewing and stood to get

myself a glass of juice, intentionally walking away from him as I answered. "Yes, I know him." Fucking Gavin.

"Do you?" he asked, pulling at his beard thoughtfully as I sat back down at the table. "You see, this man seems to have taken a certain interest in me and my pursuits. He and his staff set up cameras and the like outside the perimeter of my house today, all within city property so I could not have them removed for trespassing. And shortly after they did so, this little video clip went live."

He tapped a button on his phone and immediately, the dining hall filled with the sound of Gavin's pompous voice.

"Ladies and gentleman of Whitby, we gather here today to unearth the truth behind Sawyer Gryffin's notorious presence."

I stopped chewing, the quiche in my mouth dry and unpalatable.

"And today," he continued. "I bring to you to most pressing information of all. It seems, dear citizens that only ten years ago today, Sawyer Gryffin was put on trial for the murder of his fiancée, Samantha McGovern, but when it was time to convict him, he was acquitted on grounds of insufficient evidence. The townspeople of Whitby never accepted this verdict, however, and now, we have new evidence that might condemn him."

Gryffin frowned, his countenance darkening, as he shut his phone off and placed it down on the table. "What do you know about him?"

"Why do you ask?"

His hands clenched so that his knuckles whitened but his face remained impassive. "Why do you answer a question with a question, Annabelle?"

"I think we could keep this up all day, no?" I tossed back at him. But then my conscience pricked me. Why did I feel the sudden need to defend Sawyer Gryffin? What if what Gavin said was true? *Did* they have evidence to convict him?

His eyes twinkled, just a bit, like glittering obsidian. "Could we?" he asked.

I took a sip of my juice and shrugged. "I suppose we could, yes, but I will answer your question. I know him, yes. He's a pompous reporter who fancies himself my fiancé. I've never given him so much as a breath of encouragement to *kiss* me, much less wed me, but the man thinks only of himself."

He nodded, his eyes leaving mine and trailing over my shoulder. His lips turned down in a frown. "This is as I thought, then," he said. "He's caught wind of your being here, and has sought to attack me by spreading rumors through the media." He got to his feet and shrugged. "They'll either believe I killed her, or they won't." He tossed his napkin down on the table and stalked to the exit, his legs so long that in three strides, he'd almost left the room. "Finish your breakfast. Leave the plates. Do whatever you need to, then be back here in an hour's time." Then, predictably, "Don't be late."

I forked the remaining berry on my plate with so much force, the tines of the fork scraped along the plate like nails on a chalkboard. I bit down furiously and ate the berry, biting my tongue in the process.

"Oh son of a —" I mumbled under my breath, my eyes watering, but then I caught myself. I swallowed what remained of my juice and raised a hand to the shadow of a servant standing in the doorway to the kitchen.

"Coffee, please?" I asked, my voice wobbling a little as I recovered from the pain. "Strong, dark," *and handsome*, my mind supplied.

I closed my eyes briefly.

This was a business arrangement.

Nothing more.

Chapter Eight
SAWYER

I knew the minute I heard the footage the son-of-a-bitch reporter plastered all over the fucking internet that the bastard was motivated by revenge.

The townspeople had almost forgotten who I was, the beast who dwelt in his own form of prison, up on the cliffside overlooking the stormy sea. Now, thanks to the dumbass reporter, they'd once again think me a murderer.

The truth was, however, though I would have thrown myself off the cliff before hurting her, I was still responsible for Samantha's death.

I should have paid more attention. I should have known that she was eaten up inside, and that she was prepared to take her own life.

But instead, I'd been married to my work.

When she died, and the locals whipped up the rumor that I'd pushed her over the cliff, I wanted to leave, wanted to erase the memory of Whitby and the cliffs outside my home, but I could not.

Murderer, they said, even though I'd been acquitted. I was bound to stay during the investigation, but now, I would not leave even if allowed. I could not. I was bound here.

And now, my bitter past was coming back, just when I'd hoped to redeem my name in the media.

I stormed to my office, yanked open the door, and slammed it shut behind me. I glanced at the clock, glaring at it, hoping the sweet innocent I'd tricked into staying with me *would* be late so I'd have a fitting excuse to spank her ass.

I poured myself two fingers of bourbon to ease the pain, and welcomed the burn as I tipped the glass back. Good-quality, expensive Four Roses Single Barrel bourbon was my drink.

Who could blame me for wanting an early morning cocktail?

Everyone could.

My fingers curled around the tumbler before I reared back and whipped it into the fireplace, the glass shattering upon impact, a million crystal shards sprinkling into a beautiful pile. Broken, shattered, yet reflecting light like stars in the night sky, it seemed sort of symbolic.

But there was nothing bright about me, no good that remained. I sat heavily on the couch, noting with chagrin that no one came to hear the commotion or to see what had broken. My staff knew I was given to temper, and they stayed far, far away. I would never hurt them, but I was better left alone when in a rage. My elbows on my knees, I buried my face in my hands and closed my eyes, wishing I could buy a liquor strong enough not only to numb the pain but erase my memories.

Every night when I went to bed I'd hear her screams echoing on the cliffs below as she plummeted to her death.

It had become my lullaby...my nightmare...my torture.

I pushed myself to standing and walked to where I kept my favorite Cubans, Bolivar Belicoso, the best figurados on the market. I cut it, then walked over to my balcony, pushing the glass doors open. Below this balcony lay the cliffs. If I sat back on the little bench, I could look out over the crashing waves, losing myself in the rhythmic sound. I inhaled deeply, the aromatic smoke filling my senses and lungs. Closing my eyes briefly, I enjoyed the cool breeze off the water, the smell and feel of the cigar in my hand, the satisfying sizzle when I inhaled and the paper burned. When I opened my eyes, a flash of blue caught my attention.

Narrowing my eyes, I saw Annabelle out near the cliff.

What was she doing?

I furrowed my brows as I watched her, leaning back lest she see me here. I wanted to watch her without her knowing I did. I felt no guilt for spying. This was my house, and she roamed where she wanted to.

God, she was beautiful, her thick brown hair hanging in waves over her creamy shoulders, cascading down her back. She had a phone up to her ear, her right arm tucked under the left, as if keeping herself warm, or protecting herself. Her back was to me, her gaze over the ocean as she walked slowly, barefoot upon the grassy knoll that led to the cliff's edge. But as she continued to walk to the edge, my heart rate accelerated, my pulse quickening in my veins. Didn't she know she was nearing the edge?

I took another pull on my cigar. I needed another whiskey. I would reek of smoke and alcohol when the stylist came later today, but I did not care. Annabelle would learn this was me, this was who I was.

She stooped down and plucked a stray dandelion from the grass, holding it up to her nose as she walked along. I smiled to myself. Silly girl. Dandelions didn't have a scent. I would get her flowers that did. As I watched, her brows knit together and she crumpled the stem in her hand, then tossed it to the ground as her hand gestured wildly. I guessed she was talking to her sister. For one brief moment, I considered finding a way to listen in, to tap her phone, but as quickly as I thought of doing so I dismissed the idea.

Why wouldn't I give the girl at least a little privacy?

I took another drag from my cigar, slowly exhaling as the smoke curled from my lips in wispy, fragrant tendrils.

She didn't like me, of that I had no doubt. But I would at least attempt occasional civility.

She turned from my house and walked quicker now, rapidly approaching the edge of the cliff. With rising panic, I got to my feet, my cigar hanging limply from my hands, forgotten.

Oh, God.

I watched in growing horror as her footsteps neared the edge, her eyes skyward as she continued her animated conversation, hand gesturing to the air. She wasn't paying attention. She was going to fall right off the edge, and I was too far away to snatch her back to safety.

I broke through the panic that gripped my chest and screamed as loudly as I could so my voice would carry over the winds that whipped about the cliffs. "Annabelle!" My deep, loud bellow reverberated around me, but she did not turn. Taking in another breath, I tried again, this time more insistent, this time louder, even deeper so that I roared, *"Annabelle!"*

She turned then, one foot at the very edge of the cliff. Her whole body faced me as my heart stuttered, I crushed the remains of the cigar between my fingers, and my eyes met hers across the distance.

I wanted to pull her into my chest, to hold her close, and keep her safe.

Then I would pull her over my knee, pull that dress up around her neck, and spank her ass red.

Annabelle looked at me and shrugged a shoulder, glancing

quickly behind her again at the cliffs below. She spoke into her phone, then pulled it away from her ear and slipped it into her pocket, her eyes never leaving mine.

"Get away from the edge!" I hollered, still loud against the wind, but she seemed to hear me. She glanced casually behind her and went closer to the edge still, now both feet on the very precipice, toes practically dangling.

"No!" I screamed, which got her attention again. She turned her head back to me, staring at me a good long while before she turned from the edge and walked back to the house, whistling.

The little brat.

I needed to calm my temper before I spanked her ass.

~

I walked through the house, glancing at the time on my watch, while I went to find her. I would find her, and when I did, she'd learn that safety was nothing to be trifled with. *God.* Maybe I'd take my belt to her ass. Maybe if she felt the sting of leather she'd learn to listen.

I marched down the hallway and stalked through each room. The dining room was empty, as was the three-season porch, the library, and the second study downstairs that we kept for guests. As I stormed through my house, I thought once again what a stupid thing it was to have this many rooms for only me and the servants who resided here. It was ostentatious and I hated it, the thick carpet beneath my feet, the crystal chandeliers that hung in the entertaining rooms, the Tiffany lamps on every hand-hewn table, the hand-dyed Oriental rugs that graced the wooden floors. Every step I took spoke of opulence and wealth, and what the fuck good did money do?

She was nowhere to be found inside. The only room I

hadn't yet looked into was the kitchen. My anger mounting with every step I took, I made my way to the large kitchen adjacent to the dining area. I pushed through the swinging double-doors that led to the kitchen, noting that as I did, the chatter came to a grinding halt.

"Mister Gryffin," Beatrice, the head cook said, with a deep curtsy, her white hat keeping stray hair out of her eyes. "Didn't expect you here today, sir." Of course she didn't expect me here today. I hadn't set foot inside the kitchen in a full decade, maybe longer. I had no use for cooking or baking, and barely knew the staff that worked for me.

"Beatrice," I said with a nod. "I'm sorry to interrupt. I was merely looking for —"

I saw her then, elbows-deep in a huge floury bowl. Her eyes met mine, challenging. Twinkling.

"Hello, Mister Gryffin," Annabelle murmured. "Were you looking for me?"

Her gaze told me she knew damn well I was looking for her, and that she enjoyed making me go on a wild goose chase.

I leaned against the marble counter-top and crossed my arms on my chest. "Why there you are," I said. "I am so glad I found you. I had been meaning to speak to you privately, and was unable to find you in any of the rooms. Coming here was a last resort. Why the kitchen?"

The kitchen was damn near on the other side of the house. She had to have run there.

I tried to keep my voice calm, but I knew that she could tell I was not happy. I cleared my throat, watching her work the dough, kneading it between her fingers before approaching me once again.

"Oh, I'm sorry you weren't able to find me, Mister Gryffin." Her eyes met mine, flirting. She wasn't sorry at all.

She would be.

My patience grew thin. "Finish what you are doing. You and I need to speak privately."

I could already play it in my mind's eye, the way I'd firmly escort her to my study, push her over my desk, and unbuckle my belt. Would she protest?

I hoped so.

She lifted the soft dough from the bowl and patted it down on the floured surface in front of her. "Just a minute, Mister Gryffin," she said, focusing now on Beatrice. "So you see, after proofing, the dough is soft and pliable. Give it a good pat, and after releasing the air bubbles, simply form and allow it to rise before baking."

Beatrice looked at me sheepishly, her eyes twinkling from behind her round spectacles. "Isn't she a love?" she said with her faint English accept, wiping her hands on her apron. "Showing me how to make bread in an hour. Me mum would be clutching her pearls, that she would, setting bread to rise so soon!" She clucked her tongue and spoke to Annabelle as I turned to leave.

"Quickly, Annabelle," I commanded. She would learn to come when bidden.

I heard her turning on the faucet and bowls clinking into the sink as I left the room, waiting for her in the hallway. We would have a talk about her safety.

I turned when I heard her exiting the kitchen, noting how adorable and domestic she looked with flour dotting her nose, untying the apron at her back.

"How did you come in so quickly after being outside?" I demanded. "You were at the edge of the cliffs that overlooked the waters, and the next thing I knew, I find you in my kitchen donning an apron as if you'd been there all morning."

She laughed then, her eyes wrinkling around the edges, her laugh light and childlike. "Do you think I can bilocate, Mister Gryffin?" she asked. Suddenly I wondered if the way she'd flirted with danger had been all in my mind. Was she innocent after all?

"The apron was waiting for me by the entrance," she explained, folding her arms across her chest. "I merely stepped outside to take a call from my sister, and as soon as the timer beeped, I came straight inside and plunged right into the dough."

"Right," I said, feeling oddly foolish. "Yes, of course. That makes sense." I frowned, suddenly not wanting to look at her.

"What did you need, sir?" she asked, and when I glanced back her way, her eyes were wide and innocent.

I was crazy.

"I want to warn you not to go to the edge of the cliff," I stated stupidly. She blinked.

"Excuse me?"

"You were far too close to the edge for comfort," I said, trying to be stern but staring at her flour-covered nose, and failing terribly. "Come here," I muttered under my breath, nabbing the end of her apron and swiping at her nose. "You have flour all over yourself."

She stood stock still as I wiped her clean, her eyes never leaving mine. "Thank you." Her eyes held mine for a brief moment before she glanced away. "I am sorry I walked so close to the edge. It was so beautiful out there, so peaceful yet invigorating." She clasped her hands in front of her and her eyes met mine once more. "I...sometimes like to flirt with danger," she confessed, her voice dropping as if she were revealing her innermost secrets. "It...excites me to be at the very edge of something strong and powerful...something that could..." She paused and her voice lowered. "Something that could hurt me but won't." I watched her swallow, and as her words sunk in, I felt my cock twitch in my trousers. Was she saying what I thought she was?

I took a step closer and leaned in to whisper in her ear.

"Behave yourself, young lady." I watched her reaction. Her pupils dilated, her chest rose and fell rapidly, and the very tips of the fingers on her right hand grazed her collarbone. "If you misbehave, Daddy may have to punish you."

"Yes," she murmured, her eyes now closed and her voice hoarse. "Of course."

"Mister Gryffin?" The intimacy of the moment was lost at the sound of my name. I looked up to find Worthington staring at us.

"The stylist awaits, sir."

I took Annabelle by the elbow. "Very good," I said. "We are on our way." She would walk with me. And later, I would get her alone.

Chapter Nine
ANNABELLE

I looked at the choices before me, and felt a little dizzy. Slacks and jeans and shorts, capris, skirts and dresses, button-down blouses and peasant-style tunic tops, in every style and color imaginable lay before us on the couch. We were in Sawyer's study. "It's the largest room in the house," he'd said. "Plenty of room to spread out." He'd had a full-length mirror set up in front of the shelf where the globe sat and to the right of that, a tri-fold dressing screen so I could change behind it. But I knew the real reason he'd come here, as I watched him sitting apart from us, a cup of coffee nestled in his hands. He wanted to see every single thing that transpired between me and my stylist.

Lisa was about my mother's age, on the shorter side, with curly dark hair and blue eyes hidden behind narrow spectacles. Her haircut was short and trendy, her accessories alone likely worth my entire wardrobe at home. She wore dark red lipstick and smelled heavily of perfume. And she was a genius.

She measured me, had me stand in front of her wearing nothing but a simple sheath dress, then turned me around as if I were a cake on a turntable, taking in every curve. "You have a lovely figure," she praised.

Without thinking, I protested. "No, I don't," I said with chagrin. "My sister is thin and beautiful, but I got the dumpy genes in the family."

A low growl from across the room arrested my attention.

"What?" I said, his displeasure making my belly clench. God, he scared me.

I loved that he did.

"Not another word about being 'dumpy.'"

"It's true though," I argued. I hadn't made the comment to get attention, but because I believed what I said to be true.

"Is not," he insisted.

"Is so!"

"*Enough!*"

Lisa jumped, dropping half a dozen pins as she did. "Oh, my," she said, her voice shaking and wobbly. "I-I'm really sorry about that," she stammered.

I shot Sawyer a glare, which only earned me a narrow-eyed glare back in return.

She shook her head. "You, my dear, have a lovely figure. It is true, though, that you'd do best if you knew how best to dress these lovely curves."

I nodded. "Thank you."

"You're very welcome," she said, tucking in the arms of the dress I was currently wearing. "With just a few minor changes, your wardrobe will be complete."

"Sounds good to me," I replied. "I'm more of a mix-and-match girl myself, though," I added. "I mean, I like a simple wardrobe that I can mix up, rather than loads of clothes I don't have the time, money, or energy to manage.

"Of course," she said. "I think that's smart, coming up with a simple wardrobe. I'll give you some pointers." She looked quickly to Mister Gryffin. "Mister Gryffin has already given me some ideas as well."

Of course he had.

"Spare no cost." Sawyer's deep baritone echoed across the room. "Have at it with simplicity or mixing or whatever the hell it is you need. But don't worry about the cost."

I frowned at him. "You have to have a budget," I protested. "I can't just have whatever it is I want."

He merely sipped his coffee. His lips thinned and his jaw twitched as he eyed me, holding my gaze a full minute before he spoke. "Did I say you could spend what you'd like, Annabelle?

I grasped the edge of my dress as I whirled away from him and turned to Lisa, not responding to him.

He cleared his throat.

"No," I said with a tone of petulance, still not looking at him. Show-off.

"Okay, then," Lisa placated. "I'll be reasonable in my budget but spare no cost, and I'll keep the wardrobe simple. Sound good?"

"Perfect," I said with a laugh. Sawyer said nothing.

After I was completely exhausted and had chosen more clothes than I'd bought my entire adult life, but still considerably fewer than Sawyer had recommended, I bade Lisa goodbye.

"See to it you have what she's asked by Friday," he commanded.

Lisa nodded and trotted away.

Then I was left alone with him. He watched me from across the room, his eyes not wavering, not even blinking, as he tipped his coffee mug once more.

"It's time for you to eat lunch," he said. "I would join you but I have a conference call this afternoon that will draw my attention. I will, however, prefer to have dinner with you this evening."

There was something about the way he stood apart from me, aloof, his jaw clenched and his eyes glittering as if he were angry with me, that made me want to give him a reason for that anger. I'd agreed to obey him, but I hadn't agreed to be his little lapdog.

"I'm not very hungry," I told him. "I don't usually eat lunch. And anyway, I want to take these clothes off and put on something a little more comfortable."

The second the words left my mouth, I wanted to take them back as they hung in the air between us, seductive and alluring. Ever so slowly, his eyes never leaving mine, he got to his feet and I was once again reminded of how extremely tall he was. He was enormous, easily over six feet, his hands alone the size of saucers, the breadth of his shoulders dwarfing mine, and as he approached me, I realized that I'd underestimated him.

He placed his mug on the coffee table in a fluid motion. For a man of his size I'd half expected him to be clumsy, but he was not, everything he did was graceful and fluid, carrying himself as if he were a lion prowling the Serengeti. So taken by the way he moved and his enormity, I gasped in sudden surprise as he loomed over me.

"What were the terms of our agreement, Annabelle?" he asked softly, his feet planted apart and his arms now crossing his chest as those obsidian eyes met mine. My mouth grew dry, but I stood as tall as I could and met his gaze.

"I agreed to pretend to be your wife," I said, my chin jutting out and my shoulders squared like I was defying a teacher lecturing me in front of a room full of children.

"And?" he prompted, following his question with a raise of one heavy dark brow.

"And obey you," I faltered, my gaze shifting for one moment only to meet his once again.

"Obey me," he repeated, nodding his head slowly.

"What have I done that was disobedient?" I challenged, crossing my own arms on my chest now. "You wanted me at breakfast at eight? Done." My voice rose with my anger. He was not going to bully me into doing what he said. "You wanted me to come and get a stupid clothes fitting with a stupid stylist, even though I am perfectly capable of dressing myself," I sputtered, aware of the fact that I now sounded like a spoiled child, but unable to stop the words from coming. Lisa wasn't a stupid stylist, either, and I felt bad about that, but the very idea that I was his little toy to dress up pissed me off. "So we've got breakfast? Check! Clothing fit? Check! Stay away from the fucking whatever wing? Check!" I uncrossed my arms and pointed an irate finger at his chest. He had a temper, all right, but what he didn't know yet was that *I did, too.*

"And now I don't want to eat your stupid fancy food on your stupid *fucking* fancy plates and *you can't make me!*"

His eyes glittered with anger, his nostrils flared, and his chest rose as he inhaled. But I was not finished yet.

I jabbed a finger at his chest, poking him hard. "Fine! You want me to obey you? You want me to do what you say? Then maybe *you* should —"

"Shut your mouth." His words hissed across my chest, slithered down my breastbone and tingled along the edge of my panties. I blinked.

"I —" I began.

"*No,*" he said. "I told *you. Shut. Your. Mouth.*" He took a step closer now so the tips of his shoes were flush against mine. He lifted his hand and brought one finger under my chin. My skin burned from the heat of his touch and my eyes widened even further. "One more word, little girl," he warned, leaning in so that his voice tickled my ear. "One more word and I'll *shut it for you.*"

I closed my eyes involuntarily, my knees wobbling. I had no idea what he would do but I wanted to know. God, I wanted to know. My mind screamed *danger* and my body begged to get closer to him.

I opened my mouth. I had no idea what even to say, but I wanted to challenge him, push him, *make* him react. My hands shook as I spoke. "I... I..." I began when his mouth crashed down on mine.

This was no virgin lover kiss, but a punishment as his lips bruised mine and his hand fisted in my hair, entwining his enormous fingers at the base of my skull, my nipples hardening as he swallowed my moan. His other hand coming to the small of my back, he pulled my torso flush against the heat and warmth and hardness of his body. I wobbled but his hand steadied me, my head tilting to the side and my eyes closing as his tongue plunged inside my mouth. My body hummed with need, a vibration of arousal coursing through my limbs with the stroke of his tongue against mine. He jerked his mouth away from mine and I keened at the sudden loss, but it was only long enough for him to hiss in my ear. "I told you to shut your mouth." The surge of uncontrollable emotions infuriated me, so I smacked my palms against the flat planes of his chest.

"Fuck. *You,*" I hissed. I did not know why I was so angry, but I needed to push him, needed to know that when I slammed up against Sawyer Gryffin he would rise to the challenge and take me on. Put me in my place. I was drunk with arousal, high on fear, my body teeming with desire just from the one kiss and the searing touch of his hands. I never swore at anyone, *ever*. I was a good girl, a rule follower who crossed her t's and dotted her i's. I read books and served meals at the diner. Who was this woman shouting profanities at this monster of a man?

"You'll regret saying that." He did not yell or rage but the tightening of his jaw made me shiver.

I already did.

"I'm sorry," I sputtered, but it was too late. His hand grasped my wrist, and he pulled me toward the dark leather couch that flanked the wall. I could still see the half-moon indentation from where he sat. He dragged me along as trepidation skittered in my stomach, and I tried to pull away.

"Mister Gryffin," I plead. No response.

"*Daddy.*"

Clearly he was not in the mood to talk.

He sat on the edge of the enormous couch, sturdy and thick enough to hold his large frame, leaned me against one knee, and with a quick tug, had me belly down over his lap. I still wore nothing but the thin sheath dress and my hands floundered in front of me with nothing to hold onto.

"I told you not to speak," he said. "I told you not to defy me. You'll learn to do as you're fucking told."

My panties dampened at his words, my eyes closed shut from embarrassment. It was too much. I had to stop him. The scent of my own arousal permeated my senses as he lifted the edge of my dress and I squirmed, one hand flailing back.

"No!" I protested. "Don't! I'll listen! I will do what you say!"

He chuckled mirthlessly. "I love how compliant you are on the verge of getting your ass whipped." For a moment I thought he was releasing me as he tipped one knee up, and I shifted on his lap, but a second later, I heard the jingle of his belt buckle followed by the hiss of leather pulled against fabric. I gasped, wriggling, craning my neck to look at him. He held his thick black leather belt in hand, doubled over, forming a loop, and with the other hand he pushed my head back down so that my cheek hit the couch. He released the back of my head and wrapped his hand around my waist.

"No!" I said again, trying to push myself off his lap, but he held me tight, and without another word, the searing smack of leather met my vulnerable ass.

I screamed from the pain, writhing on his knee, flailing my arms, but another whap of his belt followed another, and then another. This was nothing like the sting of his palm the night before. This was nothing like anything I'd imagined. My skin *burned* with every smack of his belt. He would not stop. He was a man on a mission, and he was not finished until he'd punished me thoroughly.

I lost count of how many whacks he gave me, but after a good handful I stopped squirming. It still hurt, but it wasn't like the first few smacks this time. My ass was screaming hot, throbbing, and he took advantage of the fact that I no longer squirmed. I heard the jingle of his belt as he placed it down, and the next thing I knew, my panties were around my ankles and my ass was bared to him. Oh, *God!* I hardly knew this man and my bare ass was on prominent display over his knee. "Mister Gryffin!" I protested. "Oh my God! Daddy! Sawyer! Please! I will be good! *Owwww!*"

Ignoring my pleas, he'd picked up his belt and spanked me again, but this time, the folded leather snapped against my naked skin, a far more intense burn than before. I howled and squirmed but to no avail, smack after smack falling. I finally stopped fighting him. It did no good anyway. He was whipping my ass whether I agreed or not. Just as stinging smacks gave way to warmth, my head felt lighter, my whole body primed, he leaned down and whispered in my ear, "Are you going to be a good girl for Daddy, young lady?"

"Yes," I panted. "Oh, God, yes. I'm sorry." What *had* come over me?

He placed the belt down on the couch, spread his legs, and pulled me so that I straddled only one knee, my torso on the couch now, both feet planted on either side of his broad knee. My pussy throbbed against his knee, and I panted with desire as I heard him pick up the belt, but he did not spank me right away. From the corner of my eye, I watched as he held the buckle in his hand and wound it around, so that the end of the leather dangled from his huge hand. He pulled back and flicked the edge of the belt over my ass. Pain blossomed on my cheek, but it wasn't as hard as the smacks of the folded leather. It stung, but as soon as the sting faded, heat pulsed through my pussy, and I felt arousal dampen my thighs.

He reared back and snapped the belt again. My back arched on impact, my ass tingling from the sting. "Is Daddy going to have to keep punishing you?" Another smack followed another, as my need for release grew. With every smack of the belt, my pussy pushed against his leg. I closed my eyes, thankful he held me over his knee for if he didn't, I'd have fallen straight onto the floor.

"I..." I mumbled, my words slurred. "I will obey you."

The swats slowed now, a full thirty seconds between each stroke of his belt, the length of time between each *thwap* as arousing as if he stroked my clit, though he didn't touch me. My excitement mounted, as he continued the slow, steady smacks of leather on my ass. I realized with sudden alarm that I could climax over his knee just by being spanked like this. He placed the belt down next to him, and I exhaled, my shoulders slouching, relieved that not only had he stopped punishing me, but that I hadn't actually climaxed over his knee.

Probing, gentle fingers stroked between my thighs and then upward. I held my breath as he drew closer to my clit, pinching the inside of my legs before he did.

"Ouch!" I protested. "That hurt!"

"So did the spanking I just gave you." And with that he stroked me again. His fingers moved with ease through my damp folds. I'd never been touched like this by a man, and though it was embarrassing, I did not want him to stop. I *needed* him to bring me to climax. I writhed helplessly against his hand, grinding against his fingers as I geared up to climax. One hand stroked me while his second reached over my torso and found the edge of my dress, pushing the wide scoop neck down until he found my nipples. I closed my eyes, embarrassed, but he did not falter, pinching my nipples while stroking my clit. My breath caught in my throat and I bit my lip, eyes squeezed together tightly as my back arched, just on the precipice of losing control, but I couldn't. I was right there, right on the edge, too aroused to allow myself to come. I whimpered with need, a dry sob wracking me. I was desperate to come, needed release, when his mouth came to my ear and he rasped, "You'll be a good girl for Daddy. Do what Daddy says. Come for me, Annabelle."

Permission was what I needed. I screamed out loud as spasms of pleasure wracked my body. He held me fast and stroked me to completion as I gasped and moaned, panting for air. I had never come this hard in my life, and I knew the spanking he'd given me had something to do with that. He worked me over until he couldn't wring another second of pleasure from my body, and his hand left my sex and rose. I shrieked as he let loose a hard, punishing swat with his bare hand against my ass before resting his palm against me.

"I don't want to punish you, Annabelle," he said, which was a lie and we both knew it. I could feel his arousal straight through his pants, his length pressed up against my leg as I still straddled one knee. "You'll do what I say."

"Yes!" I gasped.

Another hard slap of his palm.

"Yes, Daddy!"

His hand rested gently on my vulnerable bottom. "You're a good girl," he said, righting my clothes and standing me on my feet.

When he stood me in front of him, between his knees, nearly meeting his eyes even while he sat because he was so tall, he chucked a finger under my chin and his brows lifted as he fixed me with a chiding gaze. "You'll eat your lunch, and meet me for dinner, and behave yourself, Annabelle. Won't you?"

Strange emotions rooted in my chest and belly. My nose stung and my throat tightened. I swallowed hard and merely nodded.

Thankfully, he accepted the answer.

Chapter Ten
SAWYER

I left Annabelle sorting out some of the clothing Lisa left her. Though some were on order, she had enough to start off a pretty substantial collection, and she needed some time to collect herself, I guessed. Had to be sort of weird to have your ass whipped and then to climax like that over some guy's knee.

My dick twitched.

Though I'd fantasized about taking my belt to Annabelle's beautiful round ass, I certainly did not plan on *doing* it.

Fuck.

I groaned, remembering her strewn over my knee. I couldn't decide what was hotter, the way she felt pressed up against me when I took my belt to her ass, or the way her pink cheeks flushed when she came, or the way her beautiful mouth whispered, "Yes, Daddy."

I'd burn in hell for what I'd done.

Might as well enjoy the ride.

I grabbed a glass from the side table, twisted the lid of the decanter, and tipped some in, already feeling relaxation hit my gut from the mere smell of it. I swished it around in the glass and lifted it to my lips, closing my eyes as the liquid fire burned my throat and stomach. I exhaled with a sigh when I was finished, and placed the glass on the table with a soft *clink* when my phone buzzed.

I answered it. "Yeah?"

"Meeting's been postponed for an hour, Mister Gryffin. Would you like to eat your lunch before we meet?"

Alvin's voice came over the line. I frowned. I'd told Annabelle I wouldn't make it for lunch, and now I had time. I also wanted to be sure I was home in time for dinner.

"Yes, good enough. I'll join you after I eat lunch. Thank you." Alvin knew I preferred to eat alone most days, and didn't question this.

When I arrived in the dining room, she sat obediently at the table, picking at a plateful of salad greens. She turned to face me, her eyes wide. "Oh. Hello," she said quietly, the faint pink tinge on her cheeks the only indication that she remembered every detail of what'd happened. She swallowed. "I didn't expect you here, Mister Gryffin." I noted a book with a bookmark sticking out of it sat at the table in front of her, but I couldn't read the title from where I sat.

I shrugged, choosing a chair near her rather than one at the other end of the table. "I wasn't planning on being here for lunch, but my meeting was postponed. I did, however, expect to see *you* here," I added, allowing my voice to take on an edge of authority. I wanted to see her react.

When her eyes met mine, they were compliant. Softer. "You told me to come to lunch," she said. "So I did." She did not look away, which pleased me. Though she would learn to obey me, and I wanted to test her mettle, I would not steal her fire.

"You don't eat enough," I chided, filling my plate with a large portion of grilled chicken salad, homemade croissants, and mixed greens. "For crying out loud, all you have on your plate is spinach."

"Arugula," she corrected, clearing her throat.

"Whatever the fuck you call the greens, they're not substantial enough. You need more than that."

She flushed a bit, but her nostrils flared. "And what's it to you?" she sassed. "I am not going to eat more than that for lunch, thank you."

My own anger rose, as I leaned in closer to her. "Oh, no?" I said in a mere whisper. "Did you learn nothing over my knee earlier?"

Her eyes narrowed and her lips thinned. "Please don't remind me. It was mortifying enough without having to recapture every vivid detail."

I clenched the napkin in my lap with my fists, balling it up. "Oh I'm happy to recapture every vivid detail. You will do what I say and learn your place before your time here is through. Now are we going to argue about this?"

She frowned, her brows drawing together adorably. I wanted to kiss her and spank her ass all over again. "Arguing about what?"

I exhaled. "I want you to eat more than a handful of arugula or whatever greens you have on your plate. Now I'm not asking you, Annabelle, I'm telling you...and if you don't obey me, I will spank you again, but *this* time I will not let you climax over my knee. Got it?"

Her eyes widened and her jaw dropped open. "Did you just say that out loud?" she whispered.

"I did," I said, flicking my napkin out and smoothing it over my lap. I met her gaze and lowered my voice. "Now allow me to clarify. I asked you to do what you were told. I expect you to take care of yourself. On *my* watch, I will not allow you to starve yourself. Now *eat.*"

She pursed her lips and glared at me, but after a moment,

she looked at the table and her lower lip came out. "I don't like eating in front of men," she finally said.

My anger dissolved, and I took her hand in mine. It was small and warm, her nails painted in a pale lavender, little ovals that grazed the surface of my palm. "What do you mean, you don't like to eat in front of men? Do you eat in front of women?"

Her eyes danced at that, and though she kept her left hand in mine, her right hand came to her mouth to stifle a giggle before she spoke. "Well, of course," she said. "A girl has to keep herself alive, you know!" She dissolved into laughter then, and I watched her in consternation. The girl baffled me, one minute compliant, the next full of fire.

"Annabelle," I warned, which sobered her. She stopped laughing and nodded her head. Good. Maybe the strapping I'd given her made an impact after all. "Tell me why you don't like eating in front of men." I released her hand and grabbed a croissant, tore it open with my hands, then smeared butter on it. I took a hearty bite. She watched me before she responded.

"I had two boyfriends in high school." She faltered, her eyes looking away for a minute before looking back at me.

"I see," I said, popping the other half of the croissant in my mouth and chewing it. She licked her lips and swallowed. "Go on."

She shrugged. "Well, both of them told me I was fat, and at different times made fun of me when I ate in front of them. They said their other girlfriends weren't as chubby as I was. So...after that, I got too embarrassed to eat in front of guys. I always convince myself that whoever it is watching me will think I'm a pig because I eat carbohydrates or fat or whatever. You know?"

"No, I don't know. Those boys were stupid idiots. I love

your curves." I wanted to throttle those boys with my own bare hands.

I exhaled, picked up another croissant, tore it open with my hands and smeared butter on one half. I handed it to her. She shook her head and looked away. Damn it, the girl was going to eat if she knew what was good for her.

"Annabelle," I warned, getting her attention. "You look at me now."

Her cheeks flushed and she obeyed, her eyes meeting mine. "Take this roll and eat it."

She clamped her lips tight and shook her head. I raised *my* eyes heavenward and shook my head. Clearly, she had not learned her lesson. I looked back at her. Keeping her gaze on mine, I pushed far away from the table so that there was a good space between my chair and the table. "You either eat," I offered, holding the croissant in my hand. "Or, get in trouble." She looked at my lap and shifted on her seat. Then her gaze traveled up to the croissant and she swallowed hard. She grabbed it out of my hand and took a large bite, then another, not watching me, but eating the croissant nonetheless.

"Oh, this is delicious," she murmured. I snorted.

"My staff is well trained," I said. "Our bakers came from France, and were eager to come to America and sell their wares. So they do supply baked goods to several local restaurants."

She nodded eagerly, taking another bite. Her stomach growled. I frowned at her, reached for the large bowl of chicken salad, and spooned a good dollop on her plate. "Do you like chicken salad?"

She nodded.

"Good. Then eat that with your spinach."

"Arugula," she said around a mouthful of crumbs, but she was grinning.

"Whatever," I muttered. "Behave yourself, young lady."

I rose a brow to her, and she quieted. She was learning. But she shifted on her seat again, and smoothed her napkin over her lap. Clearly, she was doing more than learning, as this morning's session had shown me. Girls who were appalled at high-handed ways didn't get off over a guy's knee, unless a part of her craved the attention. She was attracted to the way I was with her, whether she wanted to admit it or not. "Under my watch, I'll be sure you're taken care of, Annabelle," I said. "You'll eat regularly, and I'll be sure you get enough rest as well." I paused. "I think you're overdue for someone to take care of you, aren't you?"

She scooped some of the chicken salad on her greens, and took a tentative bite, eying me as she did so. For crying out loud, women were crazy. I didn't care if she liked eating in front of me or not. She would, or I'd make her regret it. I picked up a knife and sliced the croissant open before I filled it with chicken salad. I placed some of the greens on top, leaned over my plate and took a big bite, chewing well before I glanced over at her. She'd frozen with her fork halfway to her mouth, eyes wide as saucers.

I swallowed and shrugged. "What?"

"Dear God, that was the biggest bite of a sandwich I've ever seen in my life," she said, and she blinked again.

I chuckled. "Are you trying to give *me* a complex now? Next thing you know, I'll be too embarrassed to eat in front of girls."

She laughed out loud, her fork dropping to her plate. Her laugh was light and musical, her pretty eyes dancing in merriment. "Are you mocking me?" she asked.

I shrugged, and I couldn't help it, a small smile played at my lips. 'No," I said. "I'm not. Now eat."

We ate in silence for a while, and I intentionally kept my eyes to my own plate. I was, however, aware that she did what I told her to.

"After lunch, I'll go to my meeting. You're free to roam the grounds." I paused. "Well, you're free to roam the places I've told you you're welcome to go. Tonight, we have dinner prepared and will discuss the meeting with the media tomorrow. Sound good?"

She shrugged a shoulder. "I suppose," she said. Good enough.

I took another croissant and sliced it open, filling it again.

"Oh my God, you're eating another one?" she asked.

"Seriously, Annabelle, are you going to question everything I do? I am six feet five inches tall and weigh probably a hundred and fifty pounds more than you do. I need to eat. And so do you, diet be damned."

She took another bite. "Well, that *is* good," she said. "But I'm not six feet five inches and I'm not telling you my weight if you spank me all day long."

I laughed out loud. "Up for the challenge," I said, then I pretended to mull it over.

"So what are you reading?" I asked, hoping to change the subject.

She shrugged. "Shakespeare."

"Oh?" I asked. "Which play?"

She flushed a bit. "Um, not the plays," she said. "These are his sonnets." Ahh...telling. I smeared butter on a third croissant and rang the bell that sat at the center of the table.

Rafael came then, and nodded. "Sir?"

"Some dessert, please," I said. "Do you have anything prepared?"

"Certainly," he answered, leaving to fetch dessert.

"So read me a sonnet," I ordered Annabelle, plunking the remains of the croissant in my mouth.

She opened to a page. "*When most I wink then do mine eyes best see, For all the day they view things unrespected...*"

I finished. *"But when I sleep, in dreams they look on thee, And darkly bright, are bright in dark directed."*

"You know Shakespeare?" she asked.

"Not personally," I deadpanned. "I'm not *that* old."

She giggled again, hiding her face in a glass of water.

"Oh, right," she said. "I forgot. How old were you again?"

Her eyes twinkled at me, but I knew she was probing information.

"I'm thirty-two years old." I frowned. "Too old for you, really."

"Oh?" she asked, eyes wide. "I wasn't asking for me. I was merely curious. And for the sake of conversation, what would constitute 'too old' anyway?"

I sobered then. "Too old is when the young woman has more vitality than the man she seeks," I said. "Her smile and charm light up the room, and the ancient man she's with dims her brightness."

"Oh," she said. "Well then you certainly are not too old for me. So it seems you speak only in theory?"

I would not answer her but frowned. "Finish your lunch, Annabelle."

Without another word, casting her eyes on her plate, she obeyed.

Chapter Eleven
ANNABELLE

The man was an enigma to me, that much was clear. The self-loathing in his eyes fairly tore my heart in two. Why did he hate himself so? He was a handsome, well-to-do, educated man who liked control and power. He had a past that haunted him, but I did not believe what people said about him. His fiercely protective nature did not push me away, but drew me to him.

I finished my lunch in silence, and quite enjoyed it. What I'd told him was the truth. I was embarrassed to eat in front of men. It was so awkward. But it was more awkward finding myself face down over his lap, so I decided I wouldn't fight him on this one.

As I made my way to my room, I relived the memory of what had happened that afternoon, my hand going to my ass that still burned from the licks of his belt.

The mere memory made my pulse race, my panties dampen, and my breath became labored.

Why did being dominated make me so aroused?

As a virgin, I'd never had a lover. Sure, I'd been kissed and felt up, but I'd never been touched by a *man*. And there was something about Sawyer Gryffin that laid me bare, that tore my pretenses and fears asunder, leaving nothing but my own desires in its wake. He made my heart twist in my throat. He'd made me climax. He made me so very angry. I wanted to punch him, hurt him, kiss him, and fuck him.

God.

I wanted to fuck him.

If I'd been wearing pearls, I'd have clutched them.

Opening the door to my room, I saw my phone on the bedside table, and beside it, another one with a note.

"Your phone is shit. I replaced it, and the tech guy transferred all your information. But don't worry, I didn't snoop around. You do have a password on the new one, though. You'll have to figure that one out yourself."

What? The arrogant, controlling jerk!

I picked up the phone, lifted it, and reared back to hurl it across the room, then halted.

I could see it now.

He'd come sauntering in the room. "Where's the phone I bought you?"

"Oh, I shattered it into a million pieces."

If anything would earn me a punishment...

But the truth was, my phone *was* a piece of shit. It was the freebie I'd gotten when I signed up with the service plan I used, and I hadn't replaced it in years. I picked up the new one and glanced it over. The screen was larger, gleaming new, in a soft pink protective case edged in black. It looked somehow feminine and badass all at once. I wanted to see what this souped-up little number could do. I swiped at the screen, and a keyboard popped up.

Shit.

"You'll have to figure that out for yourself."

Of all the nervy things to do to a girl —

I paused, sighed, and decided to attempt the password,

hoping he hadn't set it up to wipe it out or something with too many password entries.

First, I typed my name. A-N-N-A-B-E-L-L-E.

Nothing. Still locked.

Frustrated, I typed in *let me in*.

Still, nothing. I tried Gryffin, and Whitby, but nothing worked.

As I mulled it over, trying to think of ways I could get revenge that wouldn't get me in trouble, it dawned on me. I narrowed my eyes, picked up my phone and slowly typed in the letters D-A-D-D-Y.

The screen sprang to life.

Son of a bitch.

I did not dwell long on this, however, because the next thing I knew I was glancing through my screen, swiping away, opening the apps he'd downloaded, checking through to make sure all my favorite contacts where there. Yes, perfect.

I laid down on the bed, dialed Melody, and waited for her to answer. She took her sweet time about it and finally answered around the tenth ring.

"Hey Melody," I said. "Just checking in."

"Annabelle!" she replied. "Oh thank God. I've been trying to reach you all morning."

Fear swept over me and the skin on my arms prickled with goose pimples. "Is everything okay?" I asked her in the bravest voice I could muster. I prepared myself for the worst. Mom had hurt herself. Melody had lost her job. Something awful had happened.

"Well, everything's okay for the *moment*," she said. "But Gavin came by, and things got really ugly."

I groaned. "Oh, no. What happened?"

"Well, Mom decided she was going to tell everyone that you were taken by the beast of the man up on a hill, and that you weren't there of your own accord."

"Oh, God," I muttered. I'd seen what Gavin could do. He could twist information and facts like no one's business, making the most innocent appear vindictive or malicious. It was his specialty.

"What did she tell him?" I asked. "Tell me everything, Melody."

"He came here looking for you, and Mom said you'd been taken by the beast."

"He did not take me!" I protested, but Melody was bent on making sure I got the right information.

"And then she said that you were being held against your will and threatened with bodily harm."

Oh my God!

"Melody, that isn't *true*," I said. Oh, for crying out loud.

"You know Mom, Annabelle," she said. "You know her. You know that she only gets one or two facts straight and then misrepresents the information that she knows." She paused. "But what exactly *is* he doing?" she asked.

Just like that, the memory of being stripped and spanked over his knee before he made me climax flashed through my mind. I swallowed hard.

"He's got me in this beautiful room," I told her. "He bought me a new cell phone which I'm using now to talk to you. You called me earlier and my shit phone didn't even pick the call up. This one is *amazing*. He feeds me well, and gives me free rein over his home here. The gardens are beautiful, and there are books and things."

"Oooh," she said. "That doesn't sound unpleasant at all!"

I smiled. "It's quite nice in some ways," I said. "I will tell you, he *is* quite bossy though."

She snorted. "Of course he is. He's Sawyer Gryffin. What else would you expect?"

I thought of staring at the floorboards of his office as I laid belly down over his lap for a spanking.

I sure as hell hadn't expected *this*.

"Listen, Melody, don't tell the reporters anything. I'll reach out to Gavin myself and tell him to stop. I'm not being held against my will. What an idiot. In fact, I'll be pretending to be his happily ever after wife and the whole world will see anyway."

She sighed. "Are you sure about this?"

I twisted my hair around my fingers and stared out the window at the gardens that overlooked the cliff and remembered teetering on the edge, riding the exhilaration of being on the cusp of danger while behind me crashed the strong, powerful waves upon the shore.

"Yeah, Melody," I said. "I'm sure about this."

As I ended the call with her, I knew it had been a lie.

I wasn't sure about this at all.

I played with my new phone for a little while. I'd never seen anything like it in my life. When I touched an app it sprang to life, the colors vivid and beautiful. I wondered what sort of pictures it took? I looked out my window as a breeze rustled the leaves. I'd had lunch and Sawyer wouldn't be home for a while so I had some time. Just outside the window lay the beautiful, well-kept garden, a stone bench, an ivy-lined trellis, and a pathway that led to the ocean where I'd gone earlier. My heartbeat accelerated at the memory of him, standing up on his balcony and glaring down at me, strong, powerful and savagely beautiful. I'd loved getting close to the edge, knowing it would rouse his protective instincts. I'd gotten in trouble for pushing the envelope, but hell, it was worth it.

What had come over me? I'd always been such a good girl in school, and had always done exactly what I was supposed to. My grades were perfect, and I'd gotten into the accelerated honors program without a problem. When my dad was alive we were best friends, and I never disobeyed the house rules, not even once. I never smoked or drank, and I never even had a boyfriend. I was an introvert, a loner who preferred the company of books and her own thoughts.

Then why was a girl like me attracted to a man the likes of Sawyer Gryffin? A monster, locked away from polite society in a prison of his own making. A huge, hulking, beast of a man a full decade older than I was?

A man who'd taken his *belt* to my ass?

Someone who'd supposedly murdered the woman he loved...

I swallowed, as I put my phone in my pocket and opened the door to my bedroom. He was dangerous, but being around him was like a drug. As I remembered the way he'd kissed me so hard my lips tingled, a delicious shiver ran through me.

I would never admit it, not to anyone, but there was something about him I craved.

I looked out the door and saw no one, nothing but faint horizontal stripes along the carpeted hallway, as if someone had just vacuumed, and I could still hear the faint hum of the vacuum in the distance. Doors upon doors lined the hallway, so many I couldn't see where they ended. In front of me lay the majestic staircase, the kind that tapered at the top and flared out at the bottom, magnificent enough to display a royal wedding. An enormous crystal chandelier hung from the ceiling, dozens of bubs reflecting against the crystals that hung delicately on threads, casting brilliant lights along the walls and ceiling. And to my right were dozens more doors and a thick, plush carpet. I longed to kick off my shoes and walk on the luxurious rug barefoot, to feel it bunch beneath my toes and tickle my feet.

Further down this hall was the area I longed to see, though. It was the one place I'd been warned not to go: the west wing.

And no, I would not go, even though the servants were occupied cleaning and Sawyer himself was gone on business. I was going to the garden to test my new kickass camera, damn it. I would look at the flowers and trees and sit on one of the stone benches. If I were being held here without the ability to leave, I might as well enjoy myself. But as I stepped on the carpet, a little voice in my head whispered to me.

He won't know.

This might be your only chance.

Just go quickly, and then you can go outside and he'll never know the difference.

I looked down at the forbidden wing. Why would a good girl like me do the one thing I was forbidden? I swallowed hard, remembering the exhilarating feeling of standing on the cusp of the cliff, his furious eyes burrowing into mine. The sensation of his huge hand around my waist as his hand smacked my ass.

Maybe the good girl thing was so overrated.

I would see what was down that hall, and he'd never be the wiser for it.

I looked quickly behind me again and down the stairs, then to the right. I was completely alone. And surely this place was big enough that even if a chance servant happened to be in the one area I was banned from venturing — and wouldn't that be a kicker? — I could surely hide behind a big statue or...something.

I looked about me one more time.

Nothing to see here, folks. Then I ducked down the hallway, head down, toward the west wing.

At first, it looked exactly like the other wing: a thick carpet beneath my feet, shut doors, various framed prints and paintings hanging on the walls. If I hadn't been in such a rush to get to where I was going, I'd have stopped to gaze at the paintings, as even a passing glance was compelling. Ocean scenes, mountain ranges, forests of lush green trees. Each was set in nature without a portrait in the lot, and I longed to lose myself in them. But I had no time to dwell.

Further down the hall, the air felt chillier, but I wasn't sure why. It was darker, and the lights from behind me no longer illuminated my way. On impulse, I tried a door and found it was unlocked, but when I opened it and peered inside, I found the room vacant, nothing but drapes hanging from wide open windows. I tried three more doors and found one housed a small bed with simple furnishings —a guest room? And a second was very much the same. But the furniture was covered in sheets and though the rooms appeared clean, they did not seem to have seen use in recent years. Back in the hall to the left lay a small table with a vase and silk flowers, but as I looked more closely, it unsettled me. Unlike the rest of the house, kept clean and tidy, this table was covered in a filmy layer, the dust along the edges of the flowers lending it an air of the macabre.

No one came here to clean it.

I shivered, and blamed the cold. I would see what lay down this hall if it killed me. I pulled my phone out of my pocket and glanced at the screen. I had a full two hours to wander before he came home.

I only needed minutes.

A closed door at the very end of the hallway beckoned me, and something inside me whispered, *"Here, this is where you want to go."* Like a woman possessed, I marched forward with decided steps, quicker now, my heart racing.

If he had anything to hide, he'd do so in there. I was moving so quickly I nearly ran and there was no one, no servant or Sawyer Gryffin himself who would stop me now.

What would I do if the door were locked? I wondered. Maybe I could pick the lock or something. My thoughts surprised me. I did not know why I was so determined to find what was at the end of this hall, so desperate to see what lay forbidden, that I would actually contemplate picking the lock. But I was now within arm's reach of the door. I reached for the handle, fully expecting it to be locked, a thrill of victory coursing through me as it easily swung open. I peered in the entrance. What if there were something truly horrifying behind these forbidden doors? My mind wandered to the darkest of places before I stopped it. Damn Edgar Allen Poe and his horror stories that I'd feasted on in high school. Visions of skeletons and bones danced in my memory.

Melody and I played a game when we were younger called ax murderer. We would whisper scary things into each other's ears. *If you don't reach your room in three minutes, the ax murderer will find you!* And then we'd race against the clocks, working ourselves into a near frenzy, screeching in self-induced terror like Girl Scouts telling ghost stories by a campfire at midnight.

It was really no different now as my mind played tricks on me. What if he housed the bodies of his victims in this forbidden area? What if his fiancée, the one he'd supposedly murdered, was walled up in this prison?

Squaring my shoulders and inhaling deeply, I stepped into the room. Bright light streamed through the large windows, another thick carpet lining the floor. As I looked around with wide eyes, my heart skipping a frantic beat in my chest, I began to fear something else entirely.

What if he discovered I'd disobeyed him?

Despite the fact that I told myself I feared him, my nipples hardened and I clenched my thighs together when I thought of being discovered...of being punished.

There was no other explanation than I'd gone crazy.

Annabelle Symphony did not *break* the rules, she did not succumb to a sadist's wicked pleasure, and she did *not* climax over the lap of a man a decade her senior. What *had* come over me?

A large conference table stood in the center of the room, and as I approached it, I noted it was intricately carved. I ran my finger along the edge of the beautiful, elaborate swirls that lent the table a sense of beauty. It looked like a piece of art. On the table lay the biggest book I'd ever seen, easily as big as a table for two at the diner. How did someone even transport a book of this size? I stood looking at it, and realized that it was an almanac. Each two-page layout was a map. I lifted one page, wondering at the heft of the paper, thick between my fingers, matte and richly designed. It was turned to a two-page spread of Paris, and in the columns of the map were fine details, little notes regarding population and customs, and as I turned the page, the vibrant colors amazed me. Green and browns and blues and yellows adorned each page, and there was every kind of map one could imagine, of every major city and country in the world. I could sit and look at this book for hours, and for a brief second, I wondered how long I *had* been there. Was I enchanted by this room? I shook myself as if waking from a dream, and wandered further near the window. Dusk had begun to settle, the sun now setting low in the horizon, but light still illuminated a small desk in the corner.

I wandered over to the desk, my gut pulling me, my intuition telling me: *Here. This is where to go.*

And there on the desk lay yellowed newspaper clippings alongside several framed prints.

A younger version of Sawyer, every bit as large but smiling instead of scowling, stood with a woman. One picture showed them holding hands, another showed them arm in arm, looking out over the balcony and toward the ocean. In another picture, he looked like he was high school age, dressed in a fine black tuxedo. A prom portrait? It was so hard to imagine him as younger and carefree. Who was that boy with a tux and a girl on his arm? How did they treat him? One look at the picture, and it was clear he was a child born to opulence, the cut of his tux and the car in the background speaking of privilege.

The next picture looked like it'd been taken a few years later. Sawyer was fuller, his frame larger, and the girl he was with, though the same one from the first picture, looked as if she'd aged a few years as well. They held hands, looking out upon the sea, and he held his other hand at the small of her back.

To my shock, I felt the stirrings of jealousy in my gut. I wanted to push his hand off the back of the young woman in the picture.

He did not belong to her.

Suddenly, my heartbeat revved in my chest as I thought I heard something in the hallway, but as I stood stock still, not another noise sounded. I needed to get out. But as I turned to leave, determined to leave behind whatever nightmare tortured Sawyer, my eyes fell to the yellowed edges of the paper. I knew I should have left it alone. I knew I should have left while I still could, before he found me here, before he hurt me for breaking his rules. But I could no longer look away.

Murdered by her fiancée.

My heart ached at the thought of that beautiful woman being hurt in any way.

Though everything in me said *run,* I picked up the paper as if my hands were possessed. I needed to read on.

Tragic murder the headline read, sending a chill over me.

Thursday night, authorities received a call from several sources claiming they'd heard screams coming from the cliff at Whitby manor.

Upon further investigation, authorities discovered the body of Samantha McGovern, dead upon arrival. She'd suffered a tragic fall, suffered a broken neck and multiple contusions. The authorities did not have to look far, as the man accused of her murder, none other than her fiancé Sawyer Gryffin, held her broken body in his arms when they arrived. Sources say they had to pry her body from his fingers, and though he showed signs of distress upon her death, they had no choice but to bring him in for questioning.

Initial sources say that Mister Sawyer Gryffin claims Miss McGovern threw herself off the cliff. But her closest college friends claim she was happy, had no outward signs of depression, and that Sawyer was known for having a temper. He's been arrested and is scheduled to stand trial. The family is not commenting at this time.

Tears sprang to my eyes, my throat closed so tightly I could hardly swallow, and without conscious thought I read article after article after article.

Fiancé on trial for murder of his beloved.

Not guilty.

One article after another denounced his innocence and one thing became clear: though the courts acquitted him from murder, the townspeople had not.

A large black shoebox stood to the right, tied clumsily in string. With the softest touch of my hand, the tie fell to the table and I lifted the lid, afraid of what I'd find inside. But there were only letters.

Would they be love letters sent from college? Letters he'd written to his lover?

I opened one with shaking fingers.

Burn in hell, murderer. May you live the rest of your life knowing you have the blood of an innocent on your hands.

Oh, God. I dropped the paper and clutched my throat, gathering my wits about me before I picked up another, then another. Every single letter, written by hand, no return addresses, were more of the same— reaming Sawyer out for killing an innocent, telling him that he was going to hell, hoping that he'd suffer as she did. There were even several threats on his life.

Why had he kept this pile of hate mail? Why had he ever opened it? Why didn't he throw them all away or burn them in a great bonfire?

Though he was an angry man, I knew in my heart that the accusations were false.

They had to be.

He was far too tortured a soul to have been truly guilty of her murder.

The words I'd read echoed in my mind as if I'd heard them with my very own ears.

She plunged herself off the cliff.

I would never hurt her.

She did it herself.

I was so engrossed in reading the sordid, tragic tale, I never heard anyone approach, so when the roar of his voice came to me, I dropped the papers, frantic.

"How *dare you?*" He stood in the doorway, filling the entire frame with his enormous body, his anger so palpable I could feel the heat of it from where I stood across the room. "I told you *not to come here!*" he thundered, his fist smacking the door frame, making framed prints fall to the ground, the glass shattering.

The skin at the back of my neck prickled with his fury, my heart stuttering so quickly it was painful.

"Mister Gryffin!" I stammered. "I..."

But I had no excuse.

"Get *out!*" he bellowed, coming at me then, stepping toward me with such ferocity I quaked, his hands shaking in rage as he smashed everything along his path. Vases crashed to the ground and I screamed as he lifted the edge of one table and upended it. "I said *get out!*"

I did not need to be told twice. I rushed past him, far enough so that he could not reach me and I did not stop when I got to the hallway. Pulse pounding in my ears, I ran as fast as my legs could carry me, down the stairs, through another winding hallway, and to the exit, wrenching the door open with my bare hands. After I opened the door, I paused for one brief second, shocked at how dark it had become before I ran blindly into the night.

Chapter Twelve

SAWYER

I stared at the wreckage in front of me, broken glass from the vases I'd smashed, the sideboard table splintered and broken at my feet. My chest heaved as I panted, perspiration dotting my forehead, my vision finally clearing.

She'd gone. I'd screamed at her and told her to fucking leave. She was gone.

Everything in the room but the yellowed papers was ruined. The vases we'd gotten when we traveled to China, the table handmade and delivered here from Germany, the prints from Italy and the spun glass from Mexico. It was demolished, broken, and useless. I closed my eyes against the emotions that threatened to ruin me and walked to where the curtains fluttered by the open window. She'd opened the window? I took a deep breath, grasped the ledge, and peered into the darkness. There was nothing as far as the eye could see. I ran my fingers through my hair and groaned.

You must control your temper.

This, I knew. As a child I never raged like this, but as an

adult, after the death of Samantha, my temper flared when provoked, and I left nothing undisturbed in my path.

I never resorted to violence with other people. I maintained the control I needed. I had to. I could never again hurt an innocent woman.

I'd never lashed out at Samantha, never hurt her. But as a young man ruled by passionate proclivities, I loved the carnal delight her submission brought me, and I used her to my advantage. I took what was mine, and then I took some more, never giving back what she needed. I fucked her and used her and then went off to work. She waited for me. She'd been patient, and though the doctors said there were medical complications that caused her depression and anxiety, I'd convinced myself it was my own fault.

I could not reach out and bring her back to me. I never could hold her close and prevent her tragic death, her screams echoing in my ears even now as the wind whipped the curtains at my face. And now the only woman I'd had within arm's reach for years — the one I'd held as if she were my prisoner — had gone. Once more I could not save her. Once more I could not draw her back to me and protect her, but did the very opposite, *drove* her from me. Where was she?

I scanned below my window, the light of the moon casting a shimmering glow upon the waves that crashed in the distance. I looked for a small figure running, but could see nothing at first.

When I did, the anger within me rose again, my stomach clenching with impotent rage.

She walked along the path that led to the cliff. And she was not alone. At her back were three men, and they were pursuing her.

I stepped over the broken glass and shattered wood until I cleared my path, and when my feet hit the carpet in the hallway, I ran.

Chapter Thirteen

ANNABELLE

The pitch black of night surrounded me, inky darkness broken only by moonlight reflected on the water. I knew to get back to my home I'd have to find the path, and the path that led to the village could be found if the ocean was at my left.

At least that's what I remembered. It was hard to tell from the back of a limo.

When he'd screamed at me to leave, I took it literally, meaning he wanted me to leave his mansion, but as I walked in the dark, I realized that this was a man who'd bought me a cell phone, hated that I got too close to the edge of the cliff, and made sure I ate enough food at meals. He was overprotective and fearful. He never would have demanded I leave his *home* and flee into the darkness. He wanted me to go to my *room*, dammit.

I'd been a fool. But how was I supposed to know that? And who would've blamed me for leaving?

I kept seeing him smashing the vases, the crash of broken glass echoing in my ears. His rage was a live beast, howling and snarling, ready to tear its foes asunder.

My chest hurt from running, and I had a stitch in my side that would not quit. Perspiration dotted my forehead, and the thin dress I wore clung to my dampened skin. I stopped running. He was not in pursuit anyway.

Was he?

I heard a rustling behind me, but when I looked back, I couldn't see anything. And Sawyer was the type that would make his presence known, not skulk about behind me. The cold night air rustled the skirt of my dress, tickling along the edge of my dampened skin. Goosebumps raised along my arms, and I shivered. I was freezing. I cocked my head to the side and still, saw nothing. I turned back around and charged on, determined to find the road that would lead me back to the village, to my mom, sister, and home.

I barely stifled a groan. I'd left. I'd broken our contract, and now everything he'd promised me would be null and void. I squeezed my eyes tight against rising emotions that threatened to consume me. How could I go back to what I'd left behind? My mom would have no more nurses visiting the house. Our bills would revert back to being unpaid. I'd have to go back to finding a way to make ends meet. Maybe I would take a second job. Or maybe…just maybe…if I asked him to take me back…

No. Clenching my jaw, moving toward what I thought had to be the path in front of me, *somewhere* in front of me, I kept going, kept moving. I could not go back, and surely if I pressed forward I would find what I needed to. I would figure out what to do in the morning, but tonight, I had to get to shelter and safety. I peeked over my shoulder just one last time. Though I was a good bit away now, I could see the outline of his enormous house, the windows lit up on the top floor, as if they were waiting for me.

Behind me lay some sort of twisted fantasy. In front of me lay my future.

But as I turned away from the house, I caught a glimmer of something metallic. Just about at my waist, not ten paces away, a shadow moved. I froze.

Was it him? Had he come for me? And if he had...what would he do when he found me?

I swallowed hard, inhaled, and spoke into the darkness. "Hello? Is someone there?"

I had nothing. No cell phone to light my way, no flashlight, not even the light of the damn moon. I swallowed hard and inhaled, raising my voice again, but louder this time. "Who's *there?*"

As the clouds cleared the moon, three men stepped out before me. One held a pistol. The other a length of rope. And they were coming for me.

Chapter Fourteen
SAWYER

I needed to find her. Damn it all, it was cold and dark, and where the hell was she going? Panic rose, strong and wild within me, as I raced as fast as I could. I needed to protect her.

I didn't want her to leave the fucking *house.*

I needed her to leave *me,* to leave my presence. And now she'd gone out into the darkness, and I know what I saw. Those men were in pursuit of her. Who were they? Why were they on my property to begin with? I grabbed a flashlight and my phone, and plunged into the darkness. She'd headed south, in the general direction of the town, but she was nowhere near the main road yet. With my height and knowledge of the grounds, I'd be able to find her. As I made my way toward where I'd seen her, my heartbeat kicked up. This was it. She was drawing me closer to the edge of the cliff, where my nightmares became realities, whether I liked it or not. In front of me rose sounds of a scuffle, voices, a low growl, and then I heard it. A high-pitched scream.

I'd kill them.

I ran toward the sounds, determined to find her, and

when I broke through into a clearing, I saw her, but she wasn't alone.

Annabelle lay on her back, held down by two men clad in black, while another stood over her.

He was going to hurt her.

And I was going to tear him apart, limb by limb.

With a roar that came from somewhere deep inside me, I attacked.

"Get your filthy hands off her!" I roared, crashing my way toward her. I'd never taken on three grown men by myself, but I'd try, damn it.

I lifted back the heavy flashlight and when I was near enough, I cracked it against the skull of the man whose hands were on her, the one I needed to harm first. The flashlight was easily the size of a police man's club, long and heavy, and a suitable weapon. The man crumpled to the ground, but the second man rose in his defense. His fist lashed out and connected with my jaw. My head snapped back and Annabelle screamed, but I would not be deterred. I wouldn't stop until every one of them was taken down. I kicked at my attacker and hit his knee. He stumbled forward, and I shoved him, as the third man came at me. I would not allow them to overpower me. I hit one after the other. I needed to protect her. One of them reached out and pushed her back. She cried out, and my vision went red. I saw nothing in my path but one true course, and she stood apart from me, watching with her mouth agape as I attacked one after the other, my fists flying, ducking their assault with ease, but just when I thought I'd bested them, blinding pain hit my side and my vision blurred.

"Sawyer!" she screamed. I swung my fist and leveled my attacker. The three of them lay on the ground. I fell to my knees and called out to her.

"Call for help, Annabelle," I said, before I collapsed.

Chapter Fifteen
ANNABELLE

*H*e came for me.

And he saved me.

The men who'd attacked me were unconscious, and though I could tell they were still breathing, I knew he'd hurt them. And I did not regret it, not for a minute. I knelt beside Sawyer and grabbed the flashlight he'd brought. I needed a phone. I flashed the light around his hips, looking to see if he had a phone with him, and I saw his clothing slashed, blood seeping onto the white fabric that clung to his waist. My stomach turned. How had he been injured so badly? As I crisscrossed the beam from the light, trying to see in front of me, a flash of silver caught my attention. There, in the grass, laid a blood-streaked knife.

Oh *God.*

A sob rose in my throat as I fell to my knees, my hands patting his pockets, my heart soaring with relief as I felt something hard and rectangular. I shoved my hand in and pulled out his phone, a solid, silver piece that was miraculously fine. With shaking hands, I hit the home button and dialed Alvin Worthington. I would not call the police. That wasn't my call to make. We would get him help.

Worthington answered the phone.

"Alvin? I need help." My voice shook.

"What is it?" he asked, his voice instantly on alert.

"I left, and I was attacked. Mr. Gryffin must've seen the attack from his window, and he came to help me. There were three against one," I said, my voice trembling. "I... he's..." I couldn't complete the sentence.

"Is he alright? Is he breathing?"

"Y-yes," I replied. "He's breathing, but unconscious, and far too big for me to lift."

I explained where we were, and minutes later, they came. Millie, his housekeeper and Worthington, with other people I'd never met. His staff, I assumed. They came quietly in the night. It all happened in a blur, the darkness closing in on us as the night grew darker. Finally, we made it back to his property. My stomach clenched as we approached his house.

His prison.
He would be okay.

~

"Are you alright, love?"

I blinked, not sure who was speaking to me at first as I sat in Sawyer's darkened bedroom. It was surreal to be sitting in the sanctuary of a man so scary and formidable that I'd fled his house hours ago, and even more so to see him so incapacitated. Sawyer was a huge, powerful man, and it unnerved me seeing him pale and lifeless on his bed.

I cleared my throat and looked to the woman speaking to me. Millie. She wore a bathrobe of sorts, a thin, puritanical white nightgown that covered every inch of her, her hair looped in a bun at the back of her neck, spectacles perched on the edge of her nose. In another place and time, she'd resemble Mrs. Claus and I'd expect her to come bearing a plate of cookies, followed by little elves.

"I'm fine," I mumbled, not much caring that I was being impolite.

Suddenly, Sawyer rolled his large, hulking frame over in the enormous bed, creaking the mattress, and I pulled back, afraid he'd wake up and see me in there. I did not know if I was welcome or how he'd react when he saw me.

"Don't worry, love," Millie murmured, dabbing at her eyes with a tissue. "He won't be coming to any time soon, I think."

"I'd like to call the doctor," Worthington said, his lips pursed and arms crossed over his chest. "But he'd kill me."

"Why?" I asked. He blinked, turning to me, as if he just remembered I was there.

"Because he doesn't like anyone on his property unless it is absolutely necessary," he clipped. "And his injuries don't appear life-threatening."

"Well that's idiotic," I said, my temper rising as I pushed myself out of the chair. "What if he's losing too much blood? What if one of his internal organs is injured? Did that ever occur to you?" I pushed him out of the way and lifted the damp cloth that sat on a tray Millie had brought in, removing the blanket and pulling open Sawyer's shirt.

"You're no medical professional," Worthington began, "I don't think you —"

"Well if you're going to be stupid enough not to *call* a medical professional, I'd advise you to move your ass out of the way so I can make sure your beloved master isn't badly injured."

My hands shook as he turned away from me, and Millie coughed into her hand, likely covering a laugh.

Whatever.

Worthington stomped out of the room, and Millie straightened out the bed sheeet over Sawyer before turning to me and rolling her eyes. "Likes to play the part of the master when the boss is under the weather," she muttered. "Blusters and fusses, but it doesn't amount to much," she said.

I smirked. It would take half a dozen Worthington's blustering and fussing to compare to the stern authority of the man lying in the bed now before us, but I supposed he could have fun trying.

"No doctor, then?" The flurry of activity and phone calls when we made our way back to the house confused me, as I'd only been focused on Sawyer, his pale face, his injuries. My stomach churned. They'd knifed him, the bastards. I'd been vaguely aware of people coming, and knew they were some sort of law enforcement — policemen? Marshals? I had no idea. But I knew Worthington had seen to the apprehension of the men trespassing.

"No doctor," Millie said. "Mister Gryffin wouldn't like it. And his wounds looked superficial, love."

"How did these men come to attack him?" Millie asked, pouring water into a glass from the pitcher on the nightstand and handing it to me. I took it gratefully, and gulped long, cold swallows, half emptying the glass before I replied.

I swallowed hard and didn't meet her eyes. "He was... protecting me." I cleared my throat and lifted my chin, took another long sip of water and finally admitted, "They attacked me first, and he came to protect me."

I closed my eyes, images of the knife flashing and his horrid howl of pain.

"Why were you outside to begin with?" Millie asked, her brow furrowed as she looked at me. There was no judgment in her gaze, only curiosity.

"Well," I said, looking away, as it suddenly became very

difficult to meet her eyes. "I...I ran away," I faltered. "And then when I got outside, they came for me. I don't know what they wanted. I have no money..."

Her lips pursed as she looked me over. "You don't know what they wanted? A pretty girl like you?"

When I didn't respond, she changed the subject.

"Got a bit of medical experience, I do," she said. "The good news is, Mister Gryffin will be fine. It appears he has no serious life-threatening injuries, or even anything that would warrant admitting him to the hospital." She looked over her shoulder at me. "He is lucky he is young and strong. Far too young to be held down by something as silly as a little wound," she said, her voice rising. He stirred. "Do you hear me, Mister Gryffin?"

He grunted and shifted in the bed. My heart skipped a beat and I swallowed hard. His eyes fluttered opened and then shut as he groaned. I got to my feet.

"Well you can at least give him some pain medication," I said.

"Yes, love, I can," Millie replied. "But first we need to look at *you*."

"Me?" I backed away from her. "I got smacked by one of those jerks, and I likely have a good-size bruise, but that's about it."

She pursed her lips again. "Where did he hit you?"

"The side of my face," I said vaguely, irritated with her question and uninterested in pursuing this further. "But I'm fine."

"The hell you are," came a low growl from the bed. Millie and I both started and turned to the bed, where Sawyer was pushing himself up on the pillows and glaring at me. "Let her check you."

"Well, hello to you, too," I muttered, glaring right back at him. "And I'm *fine*."

He inhaled and then exhaled, his nostrils flaring. "You'll take care of yourself and let Millie inspect you," he said, raising a hand to his face and covering his eyes, as if the bright light caused him pain. "Or when I'm out of this bed, you'll deal with *me.*"

I shivered, and my heart exalted.

He was okay.

"Fine," I said with a huff, plunking myself into an enormous stuffed chair beside his bed. I felt a bit like a child who was forced to go to bed early or eat her veggies. I didn't want to be checked, I knew I was okay, and it was ridiculous to make a big deal of nothing.

He grunted. "I'll give you *fine,*" he bit out. I ignored the way the heat of my body rose at his words.

"Lean back there, love, that's right, just like that," Millie said soothingly, gently brushing my hair out of my eyes and tucking it behind my ear. "I see where they struck you." A warm cloth rubbed against my cheek, cleaning me before she dabbed a soft cloth to dry my skin. "Some ice and pain relievers are in order," she said, then under her breath,

No heavy physical exertion for a few days, Annabelle," she said, her eyes meeting mine. "You may think this is nothing, and it very well may be, but you need to be careful not to make it *become* something bad, see?"

I knew she meant well but I couldn't help but groan out loud. She was overreacting and it was ridiculous. But as I glanced over at the bed, at the man whose bloodied, bruised face reminded me of the dangers we'd faced just a short while ago, I read the warning in his look.

I'd agreed to obey him, and he expected me to follow her instructions.

"Fine then," I said with a huff. "I'll do what you said."

Millie nodded, and got to her feet. "It's late," she declared. "It's time we get you to your room so you can get some rest. And why don't you take some pain relievers, now, before you go to bed."

As I took the medicine she offered me, my gaze rested on Sawyer, his dark eyes meeting mine as I stared. I didn't want to leave the room. We'd had a horrible argument and a traumatizing night. I wanted to stay with him, to make things right again.

I wanted him to tell me it would be okay.

Silently, I pled with him. *Do I have to?*

A gentle shake of his head, and he spoke up. "Let her stay for now," he said gruffly, his voice deep and rough with the effort it took to speak. "I'll send her to bed in a little while, but before then, we need to have a discussion."

Millie nodded and gathered up the supplies. "I'll be back to check on you in a little while," she told him. "Your bleeding has stopped, sir, and it was just a superficial wound. Bled like a stuck pig but I don't think you'll need stitches. You'll have to be sure you rest."

"Got it," he said, two fingers at his temple giving her a salute. She looked from me to him, then back again, gave a nod, and left the room. I would be alone with him. In his bedroom.

My head pounded so hard it made my stomach churn. I needed the pain relievers to kick in. God, what I needed was some liquid pain relief.

For a full minute, we sat in silence, and then I watched as the hand he held flat against his abdomen turned over, palm up, his large fingers uncurling before he reached for my hand and took it in his.

A lump rose in my throat as his warm hand engulfed mine. I felt fragile, with my hand in his, as he was so much larger and stronger. What would I have done if this had been the end for him? If they'd killed him? As I thought about what had transpired, my temper began to rise.

"You shouldn't have come after me," I scolded. "Look at you! You could've died."

His hand tightened on mine, nearly crushing my fingers. "I know you were scared, Annabelle. But I wouldn't have let anything happen to you. And if you'd stayed here, where I could keep you safe, you never would've been in danger in the first place."

I swallowed. Why did my heart race like that when he scolded me? Guilt swamped me, but at the same time, my temper flared. "I ought to be angry with you. You chased me out of your house, overturned tables like a toddler having a tantrum, then put yourself at risk trying to play the hero!"

He inhaled and closed his eyes, and I watched as his chest rose, then as he exhaled he opened his eyes, fixing them on me, dark pools of barely-tempered fury. I tried to pull my hand away from his, but he held fast. I wondered what he would say next. Would he threaten to spank me again? My heart raced as his eyes met mine and he sat up on the bed, grimacing as he shifted his weight but not releasing my hand.

I felt very small all of a sudden.

"You are right," he said. "I shouldn't have lost my temper. That part is true, and for that I apologize." He took a deep breath before he continued. "Even though you went where I asked you not to, there was no excuse for me flying off the handle the way I did. You are quite right that I behaved like a child. I'm sorry. Please forgive me."

He was apologizing? Damn it, now I had no excuse for wanting to smack him, and without anger to hold onto, I was worried that residual fear and grief might tear me apart. His eyes met mine, dark as the nightfall outside our window, teeming with emotion. And as I gazed into those eyes, I felt not just the severity of his command, not just the stoked anger at the danger we'd both just faced, but more. I looked upon the eyes of a man who was tortured, conflicted.

What demons did he battle? What voices did he hear?

"Thank you," I said in a little voice, knowing that it was too little, not enough, like a drop of water on a parched desert, swallowed up by the vast heat.

He continued as if I hadn't spoken at all. "But even though I lost my temper, I did *not* mean to chase you out of my house. I wanted you out of the *room,* Annabelle. What kind of an asshole would cast you into the pitch darkness?" He looked genuinely perplexed for a moment and I shook my head, but he continued on. "And although I was wrong to lose my temper, the truth is, you *did* disobey a direct instruction. The single restriction I gave you." His chest rose, and a sense of foreboding filled me.

Uh oh. This wasn't going so well.

It seemed my only option was self-defense. "Well, you weren't here," I said, "And I saw no reason for you to tell me not to do things."

His brows shot up so high he looked almost comical. I'd have laughed, if I didn't feel like I was going to throw up.

"No reason to tell you not to do things?" he said, releasing my hand and pushing himself further up on the bed.

Damnit.

"Wanting some privacy in my home isn't reasonable?" he asked. "But further, did you not agree to obey me?"

There was that...

I looked away and shifted on my seat.

"Look at me when I talk to you, Annabelle."

Reluctantly, I complied. I squealed as one of his hands shot out and grabbed my wrist, yanking me across his chest.

"Mr. Gryffin, you'll hurt yourself. Your injuries, you —"

"Fuck my injuries," he growled, his breath tickling my ear, his eyes like flint. "You are lucky I'm injured, sweetheart. If I wasn't, your bare ass would be over my knee."

I shook, not fighting it this time as the heat of my body

rose and my limbs trembled with impotent desire. I wanted him to spank me. I wanted to feel his controlled power. I wanted to squirm, helpless over his knee, as he punished me. I thought about a snarky response. I considered fighting him, pushing him away, but he was injured and my guilt got the best of me. I sagged on his chest and nodded my head, contrite. "Yes, sir. I'm sorry, Mr. Gryffin."

The darkness in his eyes softened at that, his brows rising in surprise then lowering. He pulled me toward him and to my shock, his warm mouth and rough whiskers grazed the top of my forehead. "It is late," he said. "You need your rest. When I am better, we will discuss what happened tonight. For now, you'll rest." He released me and point to the doorway. "Go. Go to your room and sleep now."

Sadness filled me, as if he were rejecting me after the moment we shared. How could he send me away?

I rose, bereft, staring at the doorway, not wanting to leave but not wanting to defy him again. Not tonight.

I took a tentative step toward the doorway, but as I did, I realized I was afraid.

What had happened tonight wasn't easy to forget, the men coming for me, holding me down. I still bore the marks of their attack. What if there were more of them? What if they were waiting in my room, or lurking in a dark corner of the hallway?

He could not come to protect me tonight, not laid up like this.

I froze, unable to decide how to obey him and face my fears at the same time.

His deep voice behind me warned me. "Annabelle...."

"Yes, sir?" I asked in a little voice, still not turning to him, my voice trembling.

"What's wrong?"

"I..." I swallowed, hard, as my voice trailed off. I was a big girl. I could do this. "I just...It was a little scary is all. I...was wondering if Worthington and Millie had gone to bed?"

Fuck, I sounded like a little girl afraid of the boogeyman.

Silence hung between us for a few seconds before he spoke.

"Come here, please."

My mouth was dry and my hands shook, but I turned to him. "Yes?" I asked.

His jaw clenched, the dark shadow of his beard giving him a wild, ferocious look. I wanted to sit on his lap and run my hand along the scruff of his jawline and kiss him, softening the fierce furrow of his brow and tension in his shoulders. "I said come here, please," he said.

I walked to him on trembling legs, wondering what would happen when I reached him. It was dark, and we were alone.

Anything could happen.

"Yes, sir?"

Without a word he put his hand out, palm up, as if offering me a chance to go to him of my own accord. Though his face was drawn and paler than normal, the white bandages reminding me of our attack and his injury, his presence still commanded. I reached for his hand, and he tugged me over to him. I sat down on the bed next to him as his hands gently rested on my hips, a light embrace, a touch that at once soothed and aroused me. I swallowed again.

His gaze softened as he looked at me, his voice dropping to a low, husky whisper. "Are you afraid, sweetheart?"

The tenderness in his voice undid me. A lump rose in my throat and I nodded. "Yes," I managed. "I don't want to go in that hallway alone. I know the men who hurt me and attacked you are gone, but I can't help—" I stopped, unable to continue. He released my hips and drew me to him, pulling me against the warmth of his chest.

"Sometimes, even grown women can feel like little girls," he whispered. "Isn't that right?"

Who was this man?

And how could I resist him?

"Yes," I whispered back. "Sometimes we do."

"And tonight, you need someone to watch over you. To protect you. Don't you, honey?"

I nodded, my tears flowing freely now. I trembled, the memory of being helpless and alone overwhelming me.

"They were going to rape me," I choked out, and his hands around me tightened. "They would have, if you hadn't shown up. I'd have lost my virginity to an act of violence in the darkness." My voice broke and a sob escaped, but he held me tightly.

"Annabelle —"

"I never would have been the same again," I said. "I can't imagine what horrible things they'd have —"

"Stop." His rough fingers raked through my hair, from the top of my head down to my neck, sending a shiver down my spine. "You're safe here, with me. There's no need to dwell on what might have been."

Again, he ran his fingers through my hair as I wrapped my arms around him and closed my eyes. "I don't want to hurt you."

"You're not."

We lay like that in the darkness for some time, my steady breathing mingling with his, until I rose with a start. I'd begun to fall asleep.

"You're tired," he said. "Exhausted. It's time you get some rest."

"But I really don't want to —"

He talked right over me as if he hadn't heard me. "Go to my dresser and get one of my t-shirts," he said, then under his breath, "Should be large enough for a nightshirt on you anyway."

I was suddenly very, very awake.

"Um. What?" I asked.

His voice lowered, husky now, as he instructed me. "It's late, Annabelle. I am tired, and so are you. And tonight, I don't want you to have to sleep alone."

Something in my chest loosened and excitement curled in my gut, while my eyes dampened.

Shit, I was a mess.

I gasped as his hand smacked against my ass, a firm slap that stung, but when I blinked at him in consternation, ignoring the way fire licked around my insides and my panties dampened, he merely lifted a heavy brow, pursed his lips, and pointed.

On trembling legs, I obeyed, walking in a daze to his dresser.

"Top drawer." I shivered, trying to control myself so he didn't see my reaction to his deep growl. The dresser was sturdy and well-made, dark wood that looked heavy and immovable, clearly well suited to house the clothing of the formidable Mister Gryffin. Despite the size and heft of the dresser, the drawer pulled easily when I tugged on the ornate handle. Rows of clean white shirts sat before me as his scent — musk and pine, smoke and whiskey, arrogance and manliness — filled my senses. As if in a daze, I pulled a t-shirt out and held the clean, cool fabric against my chest.

"Come here." The command reverberated in my chest, the deep sound amping my nerves and arousal as I turned to obey. A glimmer of moonlight filtered into the window onto his face, giving me the barest illuminated glimpse of his chiseled, clenched jaw. I walked to him as if in a trance, holding his t-shirt.

He would take care of me.

But where would I sleep?

I turned back to the door and stared at it. The cold, lonely trek to my room no longer held any appeal. When I looked back at him, I wondered what made me hesitate so. I had nowhere else to go. I'd agreed to stay with him, to pretend to be his wife. I'd left, but now was my chance to make it right again, to fulfill my end of the bargain and reap the benefit of his generous agreement. Stupidly, I held the t-shirt out to him, but I did not know why. What did I expect him to do with it?

"Undress, please," he said, as casually as he might have said, "Fetch me a glass of water," or "turn the light off."

In the dark aftermath of danger and pain, he was commanding me to *strip*. I took a deep breath, and then I obeyed. Off came the light cotton dress, up over my thighs, a brief pause at my chest before I closed my eyes and said *fuck it*. Over my head, and I stood in front of him in panties and a bra. I folded the dress neatly and laid it on the chair next to his bed, my eyes meeting his as he brazenly raked his gaze over my nearly-naked body. Hungrily, he took me in, not even attempting to avert his gaze or apologize for undressing me with his eyes.

"Pour me a drink, Annabelle," he commanded, his husky voice sending a shiver down my spine as he pointed to the sideboard.

A drink? I reached for the t-shirt, but his voice halted me. "No. As you are."

Oh my God. I closed my eyes briefly and inhaled, conscious of how my chest rose. Did he notice my rounded belly and curvy hips? The way my thighs touched together? Did he scrutinize every imperfection I'd memorized myself? I glanced around his room. I'd never seen anything like it in my life. It was a suite, really, more than just the master bedroom. His huge king-sized bed sat in only a corner of the room.

Behind the bed lay the open door to a closet where, I suspected, a walk-in-closet of some sort of enormous variety awaited and to the right, the door to a bathroom stood ajar. Against one wall, though, lay a desk, and beside it, a small sideboard where I could see glasses and bottles of amber liquid.

I stepped over to the sideboard, his gaze burning my skin as I walked. When I reached it, I picked up one of the diamond-cut glasses that stood face-down on the table, and uprighted it, removed the lid to the ice bucket, and scooped a few into the glass.

"Which drink?" I asked.

"Any."

I went for the one that had the least amount in it, reasoning that it was likely his favorite. My hands shook as I removed the glass stopper, and gingerly laid it on the table, the pungent sweet, warm smell of whiskey overwhelming my senses. I lifted the heavy decanter, surprised at the heft of it, and tipped some of the liquid into the glass.

"That will do."

I placed the decanter back on the table and replaced the stopper, lifting the glass and facing him. "Take a sip if you'd like," he said. Sipping from his whiskey sounded intimate and a little personal, but I welcomed the idea of a bit of liquid courage. The liquor was both cool and warm, and it burned, but I welcomed it, fire scorching all the way down my throat and into my belly. From where he lay on the bed, his lips quirked, revealing white teeth. Suddenly embarrassed, I walked to him, holding the glass in front of me as a barrier, a gift, something to distract him from the fact I stood in nothing but my new panties and bra, a matching set in pale pink satin.

He reached for the glass, his warm fingers brushing mine as he took it from me and nodded. "Thank you." His eyes met mine as he lifted the drink to his lips and drank thirstily. I watched his Adam's apple bob as he drained the glass. He slid the glass on the bedside table and gestured toward the t-shirt that I'd left next to him. "Go ahead," he said. "Put it on now. It is late, little one, and you need to get ready for bed.

"What about you?" I asked. He still lay in his soiled clothing, the expensive white shirt torn and stained.

"Dress," he ordered, as he began to unbutton his own shirt. I wanted to stare, take in the sight of him unbuttoning and removing his shirt, but I feared making him angry being too slow to respond. I unsnapped my bra and averted my eyes so I wouldn't see his gaze linger over my breasts that now hung freely, but hell, I wouldn't sleep in my bra. I lifted the t-shirt, unfolded it, and slid it over my head, intentionally keeping my gaze from his. The hem of his shirt hit me midthigh, and my arms swam in the sleeves. It billowed around me like a tent, but it felt nice, clean and fresh. He'd removed his dress shirt and tossed it, followed by the tattered remains of his t-shirt, and sat in front of me bare-chested save the bandages that wrapped around his middle. A moment later, he pushed himself out of bed, and I watched in breathless fascination as he stood, then unbuckled his belt. He unfastened the clasp, and with a firm tug, it *whooshed* free. His gaze on mine, he doubled the belt over, tucked his thumb along the fold, and snapped it. I jumped.

His brow lifted. "So jumpy, Annabelle?" he asked. "Are you afraid?"

I crossed my arms across my chest. Hell yeah, I was afraid. I was fucking terrified.

"Of course not," I lied, lifting my chin.

His eyes twinkled but he shook his head. "Seems I'm not doing my job correctly, then," he said. I squealed out loud as his hand grasped my waist and he slapped the belt against my ass, a teasing swat that still stung.

"What was that for?" I protested. He merely tossed the belt to the floor and unfastened his trousers.

"Get in bed."

I climbed into the humongous bed and shimmied my way to the very edge. The bed was warm and the pillows soft. It suddenly occurred to me how very tired I was. I closed my eyes, allowing myself to focus on the sting that still burned my ass, and the resulting pulsing between my legs. God, the man undid me. I heard the rustle of clothing as he finished undressing, and then his labored steps as he walked to the bathroom, but I kept my eyes closed. Far, far in the distance, I heard the squeak and whine of the faucet being turned on and off, but then it all melded into darkness, and I drifted into a deep, restful sleep.

Chapter Sixteen

SAWYER

By the time I'd finished getting ready for bed, Annabelle was sound asleep, her chest rising and falling as she slept in peace. I watched her from the doorway of the bathroom, ignoring the throbbing pain of the wounds along my side, the ache between my temples already dulled by the shot of whiskey, and just took in the sight of her beautiful, innocent body snuggled up in my bed. *My bed.*

What I wouldn't give to keep the girl there.

I climbed in next to her, and she barely moved. I curled up on my side, dressed only in my boxers, beside this beautiful woman wearing my t-shirt, and when I laid down, my exhaustion hit me. I snaked an arm around her waist and pulled her to my torso, tucking her against my chest, our bodies flush against one another. She sighed in her sleep but she did not wake. I lay in the darkness and held her, thankful she slept and could not feel the rock-hard erection against her ass, could not read my mind as I mentally stripped her and did sordid, carnal things to her body, mentally fucking her right here, in this bed.

Sleep overcame me. It very well might be the only night

she ever spent in my bed. I would cherish the beauty of her presence here with me, and chase the rest I so desperately needed.

~

The next morning, I woke before her, the rays of the sun completely filling the room with bright light. I could tell I'd slept much later than usual, but today I would take the day off. Hell, I'd probably have to take the rest of the week off. I typically rose before the sun did, beginning my day with international relations and meetings while the rest of the world woke but today, I'd put whatever I could to Worthington, and leave the rest for another day and time. Today was a day for rest.

Today, I woke with Annabelle in my bed.

I'd stayed on my back, but she'd rolled over to me, gently gracing one leg along mine in her sleep. She likely would have been mortified if she'd done such a thing when fully awake, and I was thankful she was unaware of how she subconsciously sidled up beside me.

With considerable effort, I pushed myself to sitting.

"How do you feel?" she asked.

"I didn't know you were awake."

"I am now," she said. "Though I have to admit, I slept like a baby." A pause, then, "Thank you."

I turned to face her. She looked younger, somehow, laying in the bed adorned in my t-shirt, her large brown eyes blinking up at me.

"For what?" I pushed to my feet, but my whole body ached after sleeping. I must have winced, because she noticed.

"Are you in pain?" she asked.

I grunted, and sat back down on the bed.

"You could call someone to fetch medicine for you," she began. "Or ask them to get a doctor."

"I'm all set," I grumbled, but she pressed on, pushing herself so she was sitting.

"No, you're not," she contradicted. "Looks to me like you're pretty far from *all set*. For goodness sakes, you don't have to get all macho about it." She frowned, crossing her arms over her chest. "You stopped a bunch of men from attacking me, took a knife wound, and you think you have to pretend it doesn't hurt?"

I glowered at her. God, my palm itched to smack her sweet little ass.

"Excuse me," I said. "That's enough of a lecture from *you*, young lady." I gave her my sternest glare which only made her eyes widen and pull the blankets up closer to her chin. "I do not plan on exactly running a marathon today, if it makes you feel any better." I blew out a harsh breath. "I will take the day off and take care of what needs to be done. And from *my* perspective, that means taking care of me *and* you."

"I'm capable of taking care of myself, thank you," she sassed.

My fingers curled into a fist as I sought to control my temper. The nerve of this woman!

"I didn't say you couldn't," I said, my teeth clenched tightly together.

Her little lip went out in a pout, and I softened a bit.

I leaned in and pressed a kiss to the top of her head. "You are adorable." Her eyes warmed at that and she lifted her chin, her lips so full I couldn't help what I did next. I leaned in and kissed her again, nothing like the punishing, bruising, heated kiss of before but gentler, softer, my lips meeting hers like a secret lover's tryst. My cock hardened as her moan slipped down my throat, her hands coming up to my shoulders, her dainty fingers grasping me as if she needed to hold on tight. I pulled her to me, needing to rein myself in for if I held her as firmly as I wanted to, I'd hurt her. Everything I'd held back galloped through my veins, everything I wanted urged me on, and her fingers snaked around my wrist, gripping tightly as I deepened the kiss. Her mouth parted and my tongue slipped inside. Her chest rose with a gasp as I moved one hand from her hip to her lower back and pulled her even closer to me. We were drowning, submerged in a wave of unbridled passion, when a knock sounded at the door. Like guilty teens caught making out in a parked car, we pulled away.

"Come in," I mumbled, my voice husky and uncontrolled. I shifted my cock in my pants, and she pulled the blanket up nearly over her head.

The door creaked open and Millie entered the room, looking as bright-eyed as if she'd had a full night's sleep. She carried a silver tray with a cup of coffee and a platter of food, and bustled in, still oblivious to Annabelle in my bed. "Thought you might not be up for coming down for breakfast," she said, sliding the platter on the table next to me. "You had quite a night. I did try to go to our guest's room, though, and found — oh!" The tray rattled as she jumped back, her eyes widening when she caught sight of Annabelle.

"Pardon me," Millie flustered, her cheeks turning pink, and Annabelle began to defend herself.

"It's not what you think!" she said, as Millie muttered something about it not being her business and grown people could do what they wanted, but it did nothing to staunch Annabelle, who went on and on about staying because it was dark and I was injured and she was afraid. Finally I could not take their jabbering a single moment longer.

I fixed my face in what I hoped was a pleasant look, but gazed at them both sternly. "Millie, thank you for breakfast. Please come back with more coffee, and food for Annabelle."

"Looks like there's plenty there," Annabelle said, peeking over the top of the blanket, no doubt wishing Millie would *not* turn back.

I eyed the platter of eggs, toast and bacon, and shook my head. "Not enough," I said, "And I could drink a pot of coffee myself."

Millie nodded her head and walked to the door. "Yes, sir, right away, sir," she said. "It'll be fine, really, nothing to worry about. I must say, sir, it is *nice* to see you up and about as usual." Her eyes widened and she looked to the bed, then she fled the room. When the door clasped shut I shook my head, poured a cup of coffee, added some cream, and offered her the mug.

"Coffee?"

"Coffee?" Annabelle said, her pretty brown eyes flashing at me as she sat up in bed. "That was the most mortifying experience of my life and you offer me *coffee*?"

I raised a brow at her and sat on the edge of the bed, taking a sip of the strong, dark brew myself. "Excuse me," I said, as calmly as I could. She really did undo me. "But coffee is the perfect anecdote after a rough night and surprising morning. Sets the nerves at ease, you know. I highly recommend it."

She merely frowned at me.

"For God's sake, Annabelle, will you relax? What's she going to do? Tell the press she found you in my bed? You think I care?" I took another sip of coffee. "But you know what, keep going on about it and I *will*."

She frowned but her pupils dilated as she looked away. "How are you feeling?"

"I'm okay. I'm in a good deal of pain, but it should subside. I can easily walk and talk, clearly, it's just going to take some time for me to heal."

"You should not be lifting heavy things or walking for the

next few days, if you can avoid it," she said, furrowing her brow in concentration. It was adorable.

"Not planning on going very far."

"You should not exert yourself too much either."

I took a sip of the mug, meeting her eyes as I thought about my reply. Under my gaze, she wilted, shifting on her sheet and looking wildly about the room before resting on me one more time.

"I think you may have forgotten something," I said nonchalantly, sipping my coffee thoughtfully as she frowned at me. "I'm the one who gives orders around here. *Not* you."

"Oh?"

"Yes," I reminded her. "So why don't you let me worry about what's going on here, and you worry about doing what you're told?"

She pursed her lips, but a knock came at the door again before she could respond. "Come in," I commanded. Millie pushed the door open and handed me the tray with more coffee and food, bowing her head without a word and taking her leave. "Thank you," I said, as the door closed behind her and she beat a hasty retreat.

"Now, you be a good girl. We'll be lazy today, and eat our breakfast in bed. In a bit, you can go down the hall and fetch your clothes."

She sat up in bed and I rearranged the tray, taking a plate of bacon and eggs and fruit and handing it to her. She took it with a grateful nod, folding her hands on the tray and waiting for me. I slid the tray onto my lap as I sat next to her, and gave her a nod to encourage her to dig in.

She took a tentative bite of eggs, and I began eating in earnest, quickly polishing off the scrambled eggs, three pieces of toast, all my bacon, and two cups of coffee.

"God, I don't know how you can eat like that," she

mumbled, her eyes awestruck and wide as she finished her second half of toast.

"Like what?" I said, genuinely curious, sipping my coffee and feeling much better now that I'd eaten.

"You've eaten three times what I have!" she said, thoughtfully nibbling her toast.

I shrugged. "Maybe so," I replied. "But I'm three times the size of you."

She snorted. "Three times? I'm not sure what girl *you're* looking at, but no way you're three times my size."

She was a perfect curvy paragon of beauty, and I grew tired of listening to her carry on as if she wasn't.

"That's enough," I warned, feeling my temper rise, hearing the curt tone of my voice but not feeling sorry. "No self-deprecation."

Her brows furrowed, she put her toast down on her plate and pushed it away. "I'm done, thank you."

She'd eaten one slice of toast and nothing more.

I picked up the small cut glass dish of fruit, and forked a strawberry, but before I ate it I reached over to her and held it in front of her mouth. "Open."

Frowning, she opened her mouth but barely.

I growled.

With a roll of her eyes she opened even wider and I placed the strawberry between her lips. "Good girl," I said with a nod. "I don't know what's gotten into your head, Annabelle, but I will not allow you to belittle yourself, not on my watch. Do you understand me?"

She started at me before responding, but finally she did. "Yeah," she said.

I skewered a large, plump blueberry and held it out to her. "Try again," I prompted.

She flushed. "Yes, Daddy."

"Good girl." I slipped the fruit between her parted lips,

and she sucked it in, her eyes never meeting mine. I read challenge in her eyes, but more, desire barely hidden within the deep brown pools. "That's a very good girl." I wanted to take her over my lap and make her squirm under my touch, painting her defiant little ass red with my hand before melting it all away, making her arch her back and scream with pleasure. I blinked. What was I doing with her in my room? This wasn't going to go anywhere. This wasn't going to be good. I pushed myself to sitting on the bed and swung my legs over the side.

"Finish your breakfast," I said, "And then it's time for you to go."

From the corner of my eye, I watched as she froze, a fork halfway to her mouth. "Mister Gryffin?" she asked. Her voice trembled a little, and it made me want to kick myself.

"Yes?"

"What do you mean go? Do you mean leave your house?" she asked, as she took another strawberry and placed it fully in her mouth.

I shook my head with a weary sigh. "No, Annabelle. Seems to me last time I told you to go you took it literally too, no?" I smiled at her. She was so cute, sitting on my bed cross-legged, eating her breakfast. Her fork dropped to her lap as she shrugged.

"I guess," she said.

I sat back on the bed and pulled some pillows behind my back. My body ached, the place where I'd been cut throbbing with pain. I rubbed a hand across my face. "I don't want you to leave," I said. "Nor did I ever. You're welcome to stay to fulfill your end of the contract, and you're also welcome to go when it's up." I found my anger spiking. "And I do want it clear that you're not leaving these premises unless I explicitly give you leave. Do you understand me?"

She nodded, her cheeks flushing slightly. She took a sip of her coffee mug and moaned. "Oh, that's delicious," she said.

I nodded, taking a sip myself. She was right. It *was* delicious. "Yeah, Millie imports that from some coffee place in Italy."

She merely nodded. "You seem fascinated with things from other places," she murmured, one delicate finger tracing the edge of the mug. "Coffee from France, chocolate from Switzerland, Italian imported cheeses and olives." She faltered, as if suddenly remembering she didn't want to carry on with anything but pushing through to finish anyway. "Why?"

I shrugged. "It gets a little boring being here all the time," I answered. "Instead, I focus on my work and have things brought to me from all over the world. I mostly make myself stay here, though I do travel to my home in Paris." I paused. I needed to find out what she knew. "Did you read the articles in the west wing?"

"Yeah," she admitted guiltily. "I saw a…little bit."

I let her words hang in the air for a moment, while I ate my breakfast. I chewed thoughtfully, sure that I had her attention. "What did you see?" I asked, sipping my coffee as if we weren't sitting in my room, barely clothed, discussing the death of the woman I'd once loved. My pulse raced. I didn't want to have this conversation.

"I…I saw that you had a fiancée once," she said. I nearly laughed at her timidity but kept my face calm, even as my anger rose without my consent. Her gaze was fixed on her plate, and she dropped her fork.

"I did," I replied. "And what did you find out about her?" I ignored the familiar closing of my throat, the breath catching in my chest as I discussed what I'd buried for so long.

She didn't answer. "Annabelle, you went into that room

after I expressly asked you not to. You decided you were going to snoop around. Now, own it."

Her eyes met mine. She swallowed, both hands by her side, but she did not look away.

"Well...the papers say that she fell." Her voice was barely above a whisper, her eyes filling with tears.

A chill crept along my spine. At her words, the scream echoed in my mind, the terrified, unstoppable scream of Samantha calling for me to help her as she plummeted to her death.

"Go on," I said, my voice strangled. I gulped a big sip from my orange juice glass, but still I could not speak. Why was I making her say this? Why did I need to hear it from her?

"I...I'm not sure what else happened," she faltered. "It was hard to understand with all the...other things in the way."

"You mean the letters?" I asked. "The condemnation from the very people who could've supported me?"

I willed myself to continue. "If the truth is what you want, then you'll have it," I began, doing my best to remain aloof, detached. I had no idea why I needed to have this conversation with her, why I needed to know that she understood my ridiculous fears about her safety...why she needed to know I was innocent. "She jumped," I said. "I was with her at the time, and I tried to save her. I tried to hold onto her, but she pushed me away. She always was a stubborn one. I didn't know what she was going to do. And yes, after she did, I went searching for her. I tried to save her, but it was too late." I finished my food and pushed the plate to the table beside me. "But that's in the past now. I just needed to know what you knew. I didn't want you forming opinions about things you know nothing about."

She nodded, slowly. "I understand." Her eyes did not leave mine. "And then after her death, the locals condemned you, though the courts did not," she said, putting the pieces together. "They didn't believe it was an accident, did they?"

My hands shook but clenching them into fists helped. "No."

"They blamed you," she whispered, her eyes widening.

I took a final gulp of coffee, slammed it on the tray harder than was really necessary, and pushed it to the side.

"Yeah," I said. "They did. Hell, they still do."

Her expression grew sympathetic, softer, as she reached her hand to mine. "Why don't you leave?" she asked, her voice urgent. "Go someplace else. Make a new name for yourself where you are not forced to hold a past you aren't responsible for?"

I appreciated the wisdom in what she was saying, but needed her to know it wasn't that simple. Outside my window was the burying ground for the woman I had loved. I could not simply leave her. It was where she met her death, and as punishment for failing to save her, I needed the reminder of that every single day.

"No," I said, not wanting to give her any more explanation that that. I could have stayed forever in my home in Paris, but I had to pay penance for what I'd done.

"But you—"

"*No.*" Firmer now, insistent, and she finally heeded me.

"Ok, so I get it," she said. "And I...I'm sorry I went into the room you asked me not to."

I nodded once. She would be.

"Are you done eating?" I asked, eyeing her plate. It looked like she'd had enough to eat.

"Yes, Mister Gryffin."

I pushed the trays to the table, and hit the button on my bedside table that led to the intercom system.

"Yes?" Millie asked.

"We're done now," was all I said. Annabelle and I sat in

silence until a knock came on the door. Millie pushed it open at my welcome. She scurried in and carried the platter away, then shut the door behind her as Annabelle and I did not speak to one another.

"That's all you need to know for now," I said. "Samantha died. I was blamed. And though the courts acquitted me and the townspeople did not, I choose to live here because I am responsible. She needed more from me. More time and attention. I threw myself into my work and never gave her what she needed. She was mired in depression and I never knew it, never understood what plagued her. But that is neither here nor there. I don't care anymore that they all hate me, but if I'm to progress in my career, I'm told it is best for me to soften my reputation." I shrugged. "So, wife, you're it."

I forced what I hope was a friendly smile, but she did not respond at first.

"I'm sorry that happened to you," she said finally. Somehow, her quiet offering of condolences helped. Something in me lifted and it was just that much lighter for a time. I nodded, my throat tight.

"Thank you."

She got to her feet. "Now I should go get dressed. I'm no longer afraid of more awful men coming back, now that it's daylight. Why *were* they here?"

"I suspect they heard of your being here from the press, and thought it would be good sport to stage a robbery of sorts. They don't like to leave me be here. I suppose it's a form of entertainment. Occasionally the locals like to come here to snoop. We're also pretty secluded up here, and someone trying to hide from the authorities could easily hide"

She shook her head. "Well, I'm glad they're gone. Do you need anything before I go?"

"Not now."

"Are you going to rest up today?" she asked, her voice sharper than I expected, catching my attention.

"Excuse me?"

"Stay in bed," she said. "You have no doctor, but wounds like that will take time to heal and it would be stupid of you to get up and leave. Got it?"

I quirked a brow. "Come here."

Her eyes widened and her mouth parted a little as she glanced from side to side before coming over to me. She swallowed, and stood about two feet in front of me.

"Closer."

Her knees wobbling as she approached, she kept her eyes on me. When she was close enough for me to grasp, I shot out my hand and grabbed her wrist. She squealed as I pulled her closer to me, tugging so hard she fell against my chest. I pressed her against me, my hand on the small of her back. She tried to pull away but I held fast. I grabbed her ass cheek and squeezed before I reached for her hair and tugged her ponytail so that her mouth parted hungrily. "I'm the one in charge here, Annabelle." I squeezed her ass again. "Not. You. Do you understand?"

She nodded, her hair brushing against my cheek. She smelled so damn good. I wanted to haul her back to bed and have my way with her.

"I do," she whispered. "It's just you're so damn stubborn and you need to get rest."

Another squeeze of her ass had her moaning out loud, and this time I could no longer resist. I pulled her onto my lap, straddling me, as I claimed her beautiful, full, sassy mouth with mine.

Chapter Seventeen
ANNABELLE

God, I wanted him. His hoarse, rough, demanding voice sent shivers down my spine. His enormous hand on my ass made my clit pulse, his promise to take me across his knee dampening my panties. And then he kissed me, and when he did, I decided the hell with it.

He was not a monster. He was hurt, mourning the loss of someone he loved, and afraid.

I wanted to make it better.

I kissed him back, and looped my arms around the expanse of his huge neck. Sawyer placed both hands on my hips, making me feel tiny compared to him, as if he held all of me right there in his hands. His tongue slipped into my mouth, and I whimpered with need. He slowly guided me onto the bed so I could now see him, all of him. He was a savage, a beast. He'd laid waste to three men with his bare hands.

And he was mine.

Sawyer hovered over me, his uninjured flank pressed up against me, the hard length of his cock against my belly. He pulled his mouth off mine just long enough to groan, "I want you so fucking bad."

I swallowed, closing my eyes as I admitted in a hoarse moan, "The feeling is mutual."

He snorted. The giant beast of a man could laugh? And then he fell to his side, tugging me so that I was flat against him.

"You ought to rest a bit," I whispered. "I'm not telling you what to do, it's just that I—"

He chuckled. Something in my chest loosened at that, hearing him chuckle and knowing I was the one who caused that.

"What I *ought to do* is whip your ass."

My heart tripped against my rib cage. I swallowed, my mouth dry, shaking my head. "Now I don't know where you get off telling me —"

"You haven't spent enough time over my knee," he grumbled. "I've been far too lenient with you. I don't think you really get it, honey." Though his tone was playful, his eyes were heated when they met mine, and so darn serious. I'd crossed a line somewhere. I wasn't sure when it happened, but I could tell that he was barely holding onto his self-control. *Danger,* my mind screamed at me. *Run.* I knew then that if I didn't leave, there would be no turning back. I was on the edge of something perilous, something that would change us both, and I had very few choices ahead of me. This had nothing to do with our agreement or the allotted time I had with him.

He would punish me. He would fuck me. And I would never be the same again.

His eyes met mine, as one hand went to my waist. "And I know if I slip my hands under that t-shirt I'd find you wet for me. Wouldn't I, Annabelle? The naughty little girl who doesn't do as she's told likes flirting with the big bad wolf, doesn't she?"

I met his eyes without blinking, my breath caught in my throat, my heart racing so rapidly my hands shook with the tempo of it. I inhaled deeply and looked at the depth of his eyes, knowing what would happen when I said what I had to. I did not even recognize my voice when I spoke, the low, seductive tone belonging to someone else who was no longer the innocent virgin but a woman with feverish needs.

"Yes, Daddy." I wanted to cry with relief, scream my victory for all to hear. I was not the wilting wallflower they thought I was. I didn't give a damn if calling him daddy was twisted and wrong.

It felt so fucking good.

I leaned in closer to him so that my mouth was to his ear, and he pulled me tight. "You would, Daddy. If you touched me now, you'd find me wet for you." I gasped aloud as he pinched one of my nipples straight through the t-shirt I wore.

"Daddy likes your answer, honey," he growled. My hips bucked of their own accord, the heat of his breath tickling my neck, his deep voice coursing down my spine.

"Yes," I moaned. Oh, God, I needed him to touch me then, my pussy throbbing so hard it hurt. I needed release, needed more than veiled threats and heated kisses and deliciously wanton promises.

The warm touch of his fingers traveled down my side, making me shiver, seconds before he lifted just the edge of the t-shirt.

Please, please, please touch me.

I couldn't breathe as his fingers grasped the edge of my panties and moved them, the warmth of his touch making me shiver as his large, capable fingers slipped down.

"Oh fuck yeah," he moaned when he touched the smooth

shaved pussy. "Bare and beautiful for me, my pretty little girl. Shit, I could come just from the silky feel of your shaved pussy."

I shook with desire, dirty talking coming from his wicked, beautiful mouth an aphrodisiac I couldn't ignore, my mind a crazy mix of "Holy shit," and "please don't stop," and the next thing I knew I was face down over his lap, his huge hands pinning me down.

My heart raced and my arms flailed in front of me. What was he doing?

His voice washed over me, deep and controlling, brooking no argument. "I was planning on waiting for this until I was better, but you're only a little wisp of a thing and I don't like having to wait on your punishment."

What? My *punishment*?

"I told you to stay the hell out the west wing. There are consequences for that." I wriggled and squirmed not because I wanted to get away, but because I wanted to feel him hold me tight. I wanted to fight him and have him win. Without conscious thought, I kicked my feet and pushed against him, and he did exactly what I wanted, *needed* him to. He held tight.

"That's enough," he clipped, the sharp tone making my pussy throb. "You'll do as you're fucking told, and you won't fight me." He yanked down my panties with one hand while with the other he anchored me over his lap. I yelped out loud as his hand connected, a sharp slap that lit my skin on fire and made my pussy throb. I gasped from the burn of it but another hard swat fell, then another, and he was spanking me in earnest now. Later, I would wonder how it made me feel so good, the burn and sting of his palm slapping against my naked skin eliciting a moan from deep within, but for now I could do nothing but feel, the fullness of my breasts brushing against his bed, his huge hand holding me tight while he spanked me. I was with a man who took shit from no one, and he didn't care if it was right or wrong, I'd call him Daddy and he'd spank my ass.

My need was rising, my pulse quickening as he growled in my ear. "Are you going to behave yourself, young lady? Or is Daddy going to have to punish you by fucking you? Maybe I should teach you to mind your mouth by filling it with my cock."

I panted, heady with arousal and aching need. I had no idea what I was even agreeing to. "Yes, Daddy," I gasped. "I'll be good. I'll be bad. I'll be whatever you want. Just don't stop." I needed to feel the smack of his palm on me, and I didn't want a little love tap that left me needing more. I wanted to be pushed somewhere further than I'd ever been, and I knew somehow deep inside that he was the only one who could give me what I needed.

I writhed against him and he held fast, another spank following another. The pain melted, though I could still feel he spanked me with as much force as he had before, now it just didn't hurt as much. My mind cleared. I could think of nothing but this moment, me strewn over the lap of the biggest, scariest, most fiercely protective man I'd ever met.

Another slap followed another, then I screamed as a swat fell on the sensitive skin of my thighs. "Open," he growled.

When I obeyed, he spanked the sensitive area of my upper thigh before slipping between my legs and plunging into my pussy. "What's your answer?" he asked.

He'd asked a question?

"I...I don't know," I said, as another hard smack followed another. Answering a question like this was like having a conversation right before I was ready to go to sleep. It took more effort than I could muster, to do much more than moan and squirm over his knee, and mentally beg him to make me come.

One final smack and he paused then, running his hand along my burning hot skin, massaging gently before lightly slapping again. "You're too delicate," he said. "I wouldn't want to hurt you." He pulled me off his lap and laid me on the bed. "I could still make you come, though."

God. Oh *God*.

"Yes, Daddy," I moaned as he pushed me back on the bed and finished peeling down the panties he'd already yanked halfway down. He tugged me up against his side before he dipped a hand between my thighs. Even knowing what he was going to do, what he planned and I'd begged him for, I squirmed, heat rising along my neck and chest.

The firm press of his fingers between my legs made everything else fall way. There was nothing now but me and him, and the throbbing arousal that needed to be put to rest. "That's a good girl," he crooned softly in my ear. "Daddy's very good girl. Do you want to come, baby?"

I nodded, my head bobbing up and down on his chest as he stroked expertly, moving along the folds of my pussy and making my arousal quicken. "Yes," I begged. "Oh God, yes."

He kissed the top of my head, and the tenderness surprised me, but I was on the edge of climaxing and the only thing I could think was how badly I needed him to fuck me. Again and again he stroked.

"That's my girl," he whispered in my ear, tickling the back of my neck with a whoosh. "You've been taught a lesson over Daddy's knee, and now it's time to make things better. Will you be a good girl?" he asked, the pace of his stroking increasing as he spoke. "Or does Daddy need to take his belt to your ass?"

Yes, God *yes,* I needed to feel the helpless loss of control over his knee paired with teeming arousal.

"Please," I begged. His strokes quickened, his grip tightened, and he rasped in my ear.

"Please what?"

I closed my eyes. "Make me come," I whimpered. God, who was I? Who was this needy girl who begged for sexual relief? My eyes still shut tight, I pled, "Please, Daddy."

"Good girl. I want to do so many wicked things to you. I'll tie you up and make you beg. I'll spank you good, then soothe the pain away, slip my tongue through the folds of your pussy and claim your sweet little clit. I'll make you get on your knees and suck me off.."

"Yes," I moaned. "God, yes."

"You promised to obey me," he continued darkly. "So when I tell you to come, you do what I say."

"Yes. Yes, Daddy."

He chuckled, but didn't stop stroking. "Good girl," he whispered. "Come now, Annabelle. Come for Daddy."

My mind screamed at me that this was so wrong, everything he said and did so wrong, but I didn't care.

"Come, baby." The last bit of coaxing was all I needed. I fell into the edge of ecstasy and oblivion, my hazy composure barely registering anything except red hot pleasure, electric vibes shooting through my limbs, my hands shaking as I held onto him, and just as I was about to come down from my first orgasm when another was building.,

"Don't stop," I begged. "Please don't fucking stop." He paused just long enough to swat my thigh.

The slap made my pussy throb. I needed more. He stroked my clit one final time and my second orgasm rode on the cusp of the first, this one stronger, harder, deeper. I shook as the spasms of pleasure overtook me, and allowed myself to give in. I needed him to hold me. I needed to know everything was okay. Taken across his knee, my ass still burning from the smack of his palm, then brought to climax not once but twice, I was left feeling vulnerable and a bit scared, though I didn't know why. Something about the way he'd brought me to climax made me want more than the pleasure, more than the ecstasy. I wanted him in me. I wanted him to claim me, mark me as his, bring me closer to him in a way he only could if he made love to me.

But I couldn't say anything. I could only cling to him, smoothing my hand over the large expanse of his chest as his ribcage rose and fell in the quiet. I hitched one knee up against him, needing to feel every inch of my body consumed by the warmth of him, needing to know that he wasn't going to leave me, not now, not when he'd laid me bare like this. A lump rose in my throat and I closed my eyes to fight against the torrent of emotions that overtook me. Without a word, he held me, his warm arms tightening around me as if he knew I felt like I was drowning, and he needed to assure me of his presence. We lay there so long in quiet that it startled me when he spoke.

"Are you okay, honey?"

Who was this sweet, kind, gentle man, and where was the tortured, savage beast who'd torn the room asunder just the night before? I could still see the rage in his eyes, the dark mirrors of anger flashing at me as he threw the furniture about the room, splintering everything in his path, the echo of his screams echoing in my ears as I fled from him. I could still hear the growl of fury as he overtook the men who attacked me, the sickening thud of flesh on flesh as he punished them for daring to touch me. And now? Now, he was a gentle lion, cradling me in the aftermath of a secret lovers' guilty rendezvous. Before he'd made me climax, my head swam with thoughts and feelings, guilt and confusion, but now very little went through my mind. I simply felt... right. This was my safe place. Here, in the arms of this man I barely knew, there was something I could not deny, I could not grasp, something that both exhilarated and terrified me.

But he would not respond to affection. I knew he wouldn't. He'd push me away. I'd seen his past, and it had killed him.

"I need to go," I whispered, though I did not move. I needed to leave before he rejected me.

He snorted. "Go where? You're half naked."

"I...I don't belong here," I said stupidly, not knowing how to express the doubts that niggled at my conscience. "I don't think I should stay." Overcome with emotion, I could only shake my head. *No. No, don't make me go. I can't leave, not after that.* "I don't know," I finally whispered. "I really don't know."

"Then don't go," he said. "I'll have to call off my meetings today anyway. It'll be a day where we can get to know each other a bit more. We can rest up. I don't have to be in any meetings until Friday."

I blinked, suddenly realizing I didn't even know what day of the week it was.

"And today is...?" I prompted.

The corner of his lip quirked. "Wednesday."

I nodded. Two more days before he'd leave me.

"Let's make the most of it," he continued. "Let's just set everything else aside and spend some time together." As he shifted on the bed, he winced.

"Oh my God! You hurt yourself. You shouldn't have exerted yourself! You need to remember that."

Without a word, he flipped me over, lifted his heavy hand and brought it down with a resounding smack against my ass. "One more time: I'm in charge here, Annabelle," he said, rubbing out the spank. "Remember *that.*"

Heat flooded my body, and I could only nod before I croaked out, "Yes...okay."

He tipped my chin with his finger and raised a questioning brow.

I swallowed.

"Yes, Daddy."

He stared at me for a moment, not responding, before his hand went to the back of my head and he gently pulled me to him, kissing the top of my head so fiercely I shivered.

Where would we go from here?

Chapter Eighteen
SAWYER

I kicked myself mentally for being such an asshole. I'd cursed myself for being too weak, and now... had I gone too far? She was a fucking virgin, an innocent, and yes, she'd walked right into my lair...

Yes, Daddy.

Fuck, I got hard just thinking about it, the words dripping off her lips like honey.

"Cancel the 3 o'clock with Bennet," I clipped into the phone, as Worthington went down the day's agenda. I had a trip coming up, and needed to prioritize. "Have you made all preparations I've asked you to make? The jet is on standby, paperwork confirmed?" My side ached from the wound, thankfully only superficial, but it stung. I ran a hand through my hair, feeling the length go askew. Ha. If the papers could only see me now -- the asshole that made Anabelle Symphony call him daddy and come in his bed. I closed my eyes and swallowed, my mouth dry.

I'd have to make it up to her.

She was in my bathroom now. I could hear the faucets turning on and off, and the sound of rushing water. I smiled softly to myself. Her eyes had grown big as saucers when she'd seen the size of my bathroom.

"That hot tub is as big as this lake I used to go as a girl..." she muttered to herself. I'd reached for her hair and tucked a stray strand behind her ear. Everything about her...so fucking adorable.

So *fuckable*.

"Why don't you take a bath?" I'd suggested.

She eyed the tub and then her gaze traveled about the room. It was ridiculous, this bathroom. A shower with jets that massaged, a shelf laden with the thickest, plushest Egyptian cotton towels. A basket of fragrant soaps and bath supplies from a client who owned a luxury beauty supply store, untouched. She fingered the basket. "I've never seen anything like this in my life," she said, her voice not more than a whisper. "This is...this is amazing."

She was in awe, and she deserved all of it. I wanted to shower her with luxuries, make her want for nothing. I'd take her on my private jet for coffee in Paris and panini in Rome, if she only asked me.

God, I was smitten, and she wasn't even mine. I made my way to where she was.

"Anything you want while you're here, Annabelle," I said, lifting a hefty slab of expensive-looking soap from the basket. It was light pink and girly, and I would never let it touch me. It was wrapped in thick satin ribbon, tied to a soft washcloth. "Go for it," I said. "Fill the tub. Enjoy yourself."

She giggled, and I felt my cock twitch. Fuck, she was so cute and I hated that my thoughts turned to little more than stripping off the t-shirt and fucking her up against the wall. Drawing that moan out of her little mouth in my bed was more thrilling than landing the biggest account of my life. I wanted to do it again, and again, until my name echoed in her dreams.

I stood up briskly, frowning, hating that I was such a sick bastard.

Her eyes shuttered.

"It's okay," she said. "I can go to my room now and leave you to your meeting."

"Oh?" I asked with a raised brow. "Don't you want to take a bath in here?"

Her gaze flitted from mine and scanned the expansive bathroom once more.

"Well, yes, but I don't want to —"

"Take the bath," I said, stalking away from her before I did something I regretted. "And that's not a suggestion."

I slammed the door behind me, leaving her to her own devices.

Sick.

Bastard.

And now I could think of nothing while I finished up my meeting except her naked skin, her soaping up the washcloth and running it between her legs, over her smooth, shaved pussy —

A crash sounded in the bathroom followed by a little scream.

I couldn't breathe, couldn't see, my gaze hazy and red as I ran. What could she have possibly done? How could the bastards have come for her? I was right next to her door, and outside the window we were three stories up in an unreachable room.

I threw open the bathroom door, thankful she hadn't locked it, and raced in, only to find her standing on the marble stairs that led out of the whirlpool tub, her hand on the shelf just above the hot tub, her mouth hanging open.

"I — I — didn't meant to *break* it," she began. Her gaze fell to the floor where a purple vase lay shattered on the tile.

I exhaled.

Holy shit, I had to get myself together. She'd dropped a vase and I'd practically expected her to be kidnapped.

"Are you all right?" I asked her, my voice sounding deep to my own ears compared to her soft one, the echo sounding in the loud expanse of the bathroom. I took a step toward her and reached to steady her. "Be careful on those steps, sweetheart. You could slip and hurt yourself. What are you doing getting out of the tub? You've only been in a few minutes."

My gaze traveled to the bruises on her arms, the ones left by the bastards who'd attacked her, and I wanted to kill them. *Murder* them. The beating I'd given them hadn't been punishment enough.

They'd hurt what belonged to *me*.

"I was only looking to get something else out of the basket," she said, her eyes lowering bashfully. "A loofah or something..." her voice trailed off, and my eyes fell to her little fingers, now protectively crossed in front of her breasts. She slowly stepped into the tub, her eyes looking anywhere but at me.

God, she was beautiful. Her full hips were curvy and welcoming, her breasts round and perfect, her pink nipples begging to be licked, and her ass...God, that ass. I needed to own it. Spank her red. *Own her.*

I swallowed, hard.

She slipped into the tub, the bubbles coming up to her chin, her eyes finally coming back to me.

"I'm fine, really," she said. "I will clean up the mess. Just please...can you leave, Mister Gryffin?"

Mister Gryffin? After I'd made her come and she'd called me daddy?

"Call me Sawyer, and don't you touch that broken glass," I said, pointing a finger at her and fixing her with what I hoped to be a stern gaze. "I'll get someone to come clean it up."

"No, I'm fine," she said, raising her chin defiantly and her eyes darkening as she glared at me. "I can clean it up without assistance, and I'm big enough not to cut my little finger on broken glass, thank you very much."

"Annabelle," I warned, returning her glare with one of my own.

"Leave me, Sawyer," she said, frowning at me. "I agreed to obey you, not be your sex toy."

My hands clenched into fists and my palms tingled, literally *tingled*, I wanted to spank her so badly. The adrenaline kicked up, and I took a step toward the tub, carefully stepping around the glass. I squatted, gathering the pieces up into my hands, piling the largest ones first. It was a clean break, but we'd still need to sweep the floor. I stood for a moment, grabbed a washcloth from the shelf, and ran it along the floor to gather the stray broken pieces.

"You're cruisin', little lady," I said, the desire to haul her out of the tub and toss her across my knee nearly blinding. "You don't talk back to me."

"Yeah?" she asked, and to my shock, I felt a wet splash hit my back. She's *splashed* me. The little brat *splashed* me.

I rose slowly, careful not to cut myself with the pile of glass in my hand, as I turned to look at her. Her hand covered her mouth, as if she could not believe what had just happened.

"My God," she gasped. "I — I don't know what got into me," she said, then she removed her hands and her brow furrowed. "You bring out the worst in me, though! Honest to God, I'm not this person who behaves like this —"

I continued stalking closer to her, the cold wetness on my back causing my anger to rise. "It's my fault you splashed me?" I asked incredulously.

"Well...well not exactly," she began.

"Get out of the tub."

My deep command echoed in the quiet. Slowly, so slowly,

she placed her hands on either side of the tub and pushed herself to standing, this time not bothering to cover her nakedness. She stared boldly at me, challenging me to punish her.

When she began coming down the steps that led out of the tub, I grabbed a thick ivory towel from the shelf and snapped it open. She jumped, but I merely waited. When she got close enough to me, I wrapped the towel around her shoulders and rubbed, then sat on a chair that stood next to the vanity, not letting go of the towel, but pulling her closer to me. I dragged the thick towel down between her thighs, careful to rub the area between her legs thoroughly. I made sure the edge of the towel hit her shaved pussy, and I did this several times until a little moan escaped her lips. When she was thoroughly dry, I removed the towel and tossed it toward the hamper. She watched it crumple into a heap before turning wary eyes to me. I held her gaze, reaching out a finger to her chin and holding it between my thumb and forefinger.

"What was the rule I gave you when you agreed to my terms?" I asked. It took effort to speak gently, but it was worth it as her eyes grew large.

"To obey you," she said.

I nodded. "And what did I tell you would happen if you disobeyed me?" I asked.

She swallowed and shifted in front of me, but her nipples peaked. Dropping my gaze to her beautiful breasts, I flicked first one with my index finger, then the other. Her knees wobbled, but I steadied her with a hand on her lower back, pulling her closer between my legs. I could smell the arousal on her, feel how badly she wanted me to take her in hand again. But I could not hurt her. I would spank her, leave my mark on her skin, and punish her for her disobedience. But I would not hurt her, no.

"There would be...there'd be..." her voice trailed off as her eyes met mine, then she inhaled and squared her shoulders. "Consequences."

I nodded. "Go fetch the basket with the soaps for me, Annabelle." I knew what was in there, what would serve my purposes well.

She licked her lips. "Yes, sir," she whispered.

I warmed at that, my chest tightening, warmth spreading in my belly at her words.

Yes, sir.

She handed me the basket. I rifled through bath soaps and salts, loofah sponges and luxury shampoos, until I found the smooth, flat, wooden handle of the bath brush I'd seen in there. It was sturdy but lightweight, likely made of pine, and it would suit my purposes well.

I removed it and placed the basket back, but I jumped when she emitted a little squeal. I blinked, looking up at her, but she said nothing. I smacked the brush against my palm and raised a brow to her. "Do you deserve another spanking, Annabelle? Should Daddy put you over his knee again?"

Her eyes wide, her mouth parted, she nodded, her pretty brown hair cascading down her shoulder and just barely covering her breasts. Without a word, I pointed to my knee.

Obedience was not an option.

"May I — could I please — well, I..." she stammered, but then she shook her head, her slightly-dampened brown locks bouncing as she did so. She inhaled, and said, "Yes, Daddy."

Then she laid herself over my knee. I closed my eyes briefly, the sight so moving at first I could not speak. She'd willingly given herself to me. She'd showed me she trusted me by placing herself over my knee.

"Does Daddy need to teach you some manners, babygirl?" I asked. She squirmed and I could see her thighs damp with arousal. *God.*

"Yes, Daddy."

I lifted the bath brush and smacked my palm with it. She jumped, likely expecting me to spank her, but I had to test it first. It packed a good sting but was light enough it wasn't awful. Without another word, I lifted the brush and snapped it against her naked ass. She squealed and her legs kicked up, but I gently touched the tip of the brush to her foot, lowering it to the ground, and waited until she lay still over my lap. I was so much bigger than she was, her hands could not touch the floor, so instead she grasped my pant leg. I'd never forget the feel of her little hands on my navy blue slacks.

I spanked her a second time, then a third, firm smacks that echoed in the large bathroom, her skin turning a fiery red beneath the unyielding wood, and as I spanked her.

"Will you do as you're told?" I asked. "Or will Daddy have to teach you another lesson?'

"Teach me," she panted. "Teach me another lesson, Daddy."

Fucking hell, there was a dirty girl in my little virgin.

Switching the brush to my other hand, I flicked a finger between her legs, satisfied that she was wet as hell for me, then pushed her legs apart even further so I could finger her. Without a warning, I lifted my hand and *smack,* spanked her pussy, lighter than I'd spanked her ass but hard enough I could feel the sting. She yelled out loud. I grabbed a towel from behind me so she wouldn't hurt her knees on the floor, then tossed it in front of me, pushing her off my lap and onto her knees. She looked at me with wide, seductive eyes, challenging me to punish her, to teach her to mind her daddy. Without breaking eye contact, I unbuckled my belt. She swallowed, her eyes falling to the leather as it slithered through the belt loops, hissing in the quiet, the soft clinking of the metal silenced when I fisted the buckle. I placed one hand on her shoulder and pulled her to me, effectively bending her over, while I flicked the belt on her ass, the sharp *snap* making her eyes widen, but she liked it, the sweet little brat liked it as she moaned out loud. My cock strained painfully against my pants, but I needed her to feel the taste of leather just one more time before I punished her more. Another flick of the belt brought a satisfying red stripe across her ass. I dropped the belt and she sighed.

"You want more, little girl?" I asked. She nodded, her head bobbing between my thighs. Fuck, she wanted me to whip her ass.

I would.

But first, she'd learn to obey me.

"You ever given a man a blow job, honey?" I asked. I loved that she was a virgin, and knew as the words left my mouth I never should have asked them, because if she confessed to blowing another guy, I'd have to find him and kill him.

She shook her head from side by side.

"It's my job to teach you lots of things, then," I said, unzipping my pants. Her eyes widened as I removed my cock and tickled her lips with the tip. "Open wide, honey. Time for you to learn another lesson."

She licked the tip and for a moment I wondered if she'd lied to me. The girl was a natural. Just the right amount of pressure, just the right amount of suction, and my head fell back as she suckled and licked my cock.

"Fuck, baby," I said, my voice strangled and hoarse. "Holy fuck."

She smiled around my cock, the prettiest thing I'd ever seen, still sucking, her eagerness to please me making me even harder. I gently twirled my hands in her hair and tugged. Her lids fell to half-mast and I nearly lost it. I fucked her mouth then, thrusting in and out hard enough to make her eyes water, but not hard enough to make her hurt. She gasped but did not release me. Although my orgasm was building, first and foremost, I had to take care of her. I couldn't harm her. Though it took every bit of my self-control, I finally pulled out. She whimpered a little and her expression saddened.

"I didn't do a good enough job?" she whispered, as pretty and fetching as a kitten.

"Baby," I said, smoothing my hand along the top of her head. "That was so fucking good I was gonna blow in your mouth. I can't do that to you. Not now. Not yet. You're too new."

"Oh." Her face fell.

I'd let her down by not letting her swallow?

Jesus.

"Soon, baby," I said. "Soon, you'll have it all."

She nodded then, her eyes warming at that. "Yes, Daddy."

I wanted to fuck her so badly I could taste it, but I couldn't take advantage of her. I'd take a quick shower and take care of business and move on with my day.

I would not fuck her. Not yet. *No.*

But even as I scolded myself, I knew. I was a goner.

A sick, twisted, fucking goner.

Chapter Nineteen
ANNABELLE

I didn't know what came over me. This was *crazy*.

I was a virgin, never even had missionary sex before, and here I was on my knees sucking off the hottest, richest, dirtiest guy I'd ever met. My ass burned from the lashes of his belt, my skin on fire from being *spanked* by him.

And I liked it.

It was so wrong, and so delicious. And now I wanted more of him. I craved him like a starving woman craves food. One taste simply wasn't enough.

"Go," he said to me, jarring me from my thoughts. "Be careful walking on the floor until someone comes to clean it up, and go back to your room. We need to talk."

Those words settled in my stomach.

We need to talk.

What did we need to talk about?

I reached for a towel, but he was too quick. He took the one he'd already gotten for me and draped it about my shoulders, tucking it in around me before placing a gentle kiss on my forehead and leading me out of the bathroom. "Go on and get dressed." His eyes twinkled a bit, and I wondered why.

Delicious anticipation wove through me, and I turned to the door.

"Yes, Daddy," I said over my shoulder. I opened the door with a trembling hand. Even the *door knob* felt expensive, the carpet beneath my feet, the thick towel wrapped around me.

How rich *was* he?

Billionaire, the papers said. He wanted for nothing.

But if that were really true, I mused, my bare feet padding along the thick, plush carpet...then why did he want me?

～

When I arrived in my room, I stood in the doorway, the towel falling off one shoulder, barely covering me. I stood, and stared.

A brass fixture sat in the center of the room with wheels on the bottom and hooks at the top, like a temporary wardrobe or something they might have for actors or people stocking shelves in stores.

Beautiful, luxurious, exquisite clothes hung from hangers.

All my size. All *amazing*.

I walked toward them like I was dreaming, my hand outstretched as if they'd disappear if I blinked. Glimmering golds and reds, a silvery satin with a pearl neckline, and boxes upon boxes lined up to the right of the closet. With trembling hands, I lifted one lid, my jaw dropping. Shoes, of every style imaginable. One glimpse and I knew one shoe alone would pay my rent for a year. I touched the buttery Italian leather and lifted one tan-colored platform, sniffing the rich leather. Oh, *my*.

A white folded note caught my eye. Placing the shoe back in the box, I reached for the note, and opened it, the towel falling to the floor. I stood naked in the room, the touch of his belt still stinging on my skin, awed by the luxury in my midst.

I have a business meeting I could not cancel, tomorrow morning, in Paris.

I'd like to take you on my private jet tonight.

Please choose something to wear that's comfortable in the wardrobe, and pack a dress and shoes, whichever you'd like best.

Paris.

Paris!

Oh my freaking God. This was the stuff that dreams were made of. Was he ready to travel already? So soon after being injured?

I smirked. As if I could do a damn thing about it. He'd do what he wanted regardless.

I fingered the soft, supple fabric of a pretty red dress. Muted colors and drab, loose-fitting clothes were easy to find at the thrift store. These bold colors and low-cut necklines shocked me. Was he out of his mind? Where was the simple little black or gray dress I'd feel comfortable in? I eyed the shoes with disdain, scowling at them as if they would bite me.

"I'd fall and break my ankle wearing you," I muttered at one lovely but death-defying pair.

"I'd catch you."

I screamed, snatching at the towel on the floor as I spun to stare at Sawyer in the doorway. He was dressed in an elegant, well-cut charcoal gray suit, and he looked so good my mouth practically began to water. His broad shoulders filled the doorway, his narrower hips pushed up against one side as he lifted a glass to his lips, amber liquid, ice clinking as he sipped. Ankles crossed, he was the picture of rich, casual perfection.

I swallowed. "You want me to wear heels like this?" I asked.

He shrugged. "I don't much care what you wear for heels,"

he answered. "Anything here can be returned. Lisa picked them out for you. But if you're not comfortable in them, I won't push it."

I'd catch you.

I had the sudden ridiculous notion of me tripping, going flying, and him snagging me about the waist and righting me on a cobblestoned street corner in Paris.

Craziness.

I glanced back at the shoes and realized there were lower-heeled numbers, though they all looked expensive and luxurious.

"Alrighty then," I muttered. "But I don't know about these dresses, Mister —"

"What'd I say about my name?" His chiding tone arrested me mid-sentence. When I stared back at him, I felt my tummy flutter at his stern, dark look, brows furrowed over eyes that looked black as coal, jaw lined in dark scruff, lips thinned, one hand on his hip. He'd whipped my ass with the tail end of his belt, and my skin still burned from the spanking he'd given me. He would spank me if he wanted to.

I fucking loved that he would.

My tummy dropped and my clit throbbed.

I cleared my throat. "You said to call you Sawyer," I said, meeting his gaze.

He nodded. "Those dresses are custom-fit for you, Annabelle." With the hand holding his glass, he pointed at the dresses. "You have an hourglass figure, and my stylist knows what type of clothing would best fit your body type. Jewel colors and warmer tones suit you, as well as halter and sweetheart necklines."

What was a sweetheart neckline?

I swallowed. "Hourglass body type?" I asked. *Bullshit*, hourglass body type. I had full hips and a rounded tummy, and I was hardly Marilyn Monroe.

He nodded soberly. "Yes. Hourglass. That means your waist is narrower than your hips and bust."

He was a fashion expert?

"How do you know that?"

His eyes twinkled at me, just slightly, enough to make my belly warm a little. "I sell clothing, sweetheart," he said. "You didn't know that?"

I felt a faint flush creep along my cheeks and neck. How could I have practically slept with the man and not known that? I cleared my throat. "Um. Well, no, sorry. I didn't know that. So, do you design them, too?"

He shook his head. "No. I have teams that manage all that. But to be successful, I need to know the market, and I know it well. I know what your body type is, what colors look good on you, and what you should avoid. And I'm telling you that every one of the items will suit you perfectly." He nodded to the clothing rack. "Try them on. You'll see."

Still clutching the towel, I walked back over to the clothes and choose the simplest of them all, a deep burgundy wrap dress with a low v-neck. It gathered at the waist, the hem slightly angled. I glanced around and found bras and panties neatly stacked atop my dresser. "I'll try this one," I said. "Will you please leave?"

I half expected him to balk at that, but to his credit, he gave me one long look before reaching for the doorknob, and pulling it shut tight behind him.

As soon as he left, I dropped the towel, grabbed the dress, and ran over to the mirror.

Was he right? *Would* they all look good on me? For someone who'd been on a shoestring budget for over a decade, who considered swimsuit shopping a medieval form of torture, high-end, expensive clothing was an exciting prospect. I tried on the burgundy, and gasped when the material draped to my knees.

I. Looked. *Amazing*.

My breasts were full and curvy, my waist slimmed with the cinched material, the color making me look vibrant and alive. My eyes even looked brighter. Holy *shit*.

Pulling that garment off and placing it on the bed, I then tried on an olive-green number with scooped neckline, a shorter dress but still gorgeous. I sighed dreamily, feeling like I'd just stepped off a runway. Maybe I *would* wear those damn heels after all. I tossed that off and slipped on a v-neck halter top gold dress that shimmered all the way down to my ankles. Jesus, was he taking me to the Oscars or something? But I stared at my reflection, mouth hanging open, as I gazed at the way the material hugged my curves, accentuating my slimmer waist, and shined like stars in the night sky. A gentle knock startled me just seconds before Sawyer pushed the door open.

He whistled low, and I smiled. He liked it.

"You look fucking gorgeous," he said, his eyes smoldering. "Wear *that* one."

"This one?" I croaked. It was the most expensive, extravagant thing that had ever graced my body.

"That one," he repeated. "I have someone who will fix your hair and make-up if you'd like.

I nodded. I mean, slapping on drugstore lipstick and a messy bun wasn't going to do the trick.

"Okay, Sawyer, how much does this thing *cost?*"

"You don't need to know that."

I pursed my lips and raised my brows, but he only narrowed his eyes at me. I humphed and he crossed his arms on his chest.

"Doesn't matter how much it cost," he said. "It could be three million, and I'd still figure out how to lift it up to bare your ass."

I tingled from head to toe. "No doubt," I muttered, and at that he laughed, actually *laughed* out loud.

I blinked. "Are you laughing at me?"

He shook his head. "Not at you, sweetheart. You're just fucking adorable. Now pick out some shoes and I'll send the girl in to do your hair and make-up."

I swallowed, meeting his gaze, and I said the only sensible thing I could. "Yes, sir."

Chapter Twenty

SAWYER

When she finally came to me, I stared at her as if she were a mirage, or better, an angel from a dream. Demons came to me in my dreams... but here stood a beautiful angel.

She was dressed in my top line of exquisite evening gowns, hand sewn and custom-made, and she looked like an absolute dream. Her hair hung softly about her shoulders in waves. Her eyes were bright, her complexion clear, and the dress...God, if I could fuck her with my eyes, she'd be up against the wall at this very moment, that dress up around her waist.

I cleared my throat. "You look...gorgeous." My voice was husky and broken, colored by the emotions that teemed within me. I wanted to own her, and she'd barely even begun calling me by name.

Annabelle cast her eyes to the floor and shifted, shy from the praise. "Thank you."

"Come, join me for dinner tonight. I've ordered an elegant meal for two, and after that I'll have you pack a bag. My business meeting is early tomorrow morning in Paris, but with the time difference, we'll have to leave shortly after dinner."

Her gaze returned to mine, her eyes expectant like a little girl on her birthday. "You're really taking me to Paris?" she asked, her voice rising in excitement.

I couldn't help but smile at her. "Of course. Did you think I was joking in my note?"

"I...I wasn't sure." She clapped her hands, the cutest damn thing I'd ever seen. "Oh, thank you," she said, then her brows furrowed. "What about my passport and things like that?"

"Taken care of," I said with a smile.

"Thank you, Mist— Sawyer. Thank you." She raced across the room and threw her arms around my neck, standing on her tippy toes, and even then she barely reached me. My arms encircled her waist and I held on tight, closing my eyes for a moment to enjoy the wonder of this moment, holding the girl in my arms, her thanks still ringing in my ears.

"You're very welcome. Now come to dinner," I said, pulling away with some reluctance.

"Would you like a glass of wine or sherry?"

She went to pull out her chair and I stopped her by placing one firm hand on the arch of the chair. "I do that, Annabelle."

Her cheeks flushed slightly as she nodded and stepped back, giving me room to move the chair out. I raised a hand to signal for my wait staff to join us, and on cue, a white-coated gentleman came to do my bidding, bowing to me as he walked our way.

"Sir?" he asked.

"A drink for the lady, please," I said, nodding to Annabelle. "What's your drink tonight, honey?"

"Straight vodka," she mumbled.

I shook my head. "Bring a bottle of one of those white zinfandels I purchased last month. Ok?"

"Yes, sir," he said, and he took his leave.

"Now," I said, pulling my chair out beside hers and gently rubbing her back. She sighed as my hand smoothed over the soft fabric. "Take a moment to compose yourself. Then we'll talk. Whatever it is will keep."

She took a deep breath in, then exhaled, straightening her shoulders. In no time at all, our waiter appeared with a chilled bottle of white and poured us two glasses.

"Here you are, sir," he said. "We can either do appetizers, or go straight to the main course."

"Just the main course, please," I ordered, concerned about time. Annabelle took the glass offered to her gratefully, and tilted it back, easily drinking half her glass in one gulp. I signaled to our waiter, who filled the glass without a word, then silently took his leave as she took another sip.

"Have something to eat with that wine," I said. "Drinking on an empty stomach is not a good idea."

"Sounds to me like an *amazing* idea," she huffed. "I think I can handle it."

I growled without even realizing I had. She blinked up at me. "Oh," she said. "Oh, my." But she obediently put her glass down, and thankfully the wait staff showed up with several large platters of food.

Annabelle plucked an olive off a toothpick, and ate it. "Ooooh," she hummed. "These are delicious. Where do they come from?"

"Tuscany," I replied. "They're marinated in olive oil. I'm glad you like them."

"I love them," she said, her mouth stuffed full of olives. I watched, pleased, as she took another sip of her wine, and our waiters brought out a platter of warm bread and olive oil. "These are delicious." Her words were slurred, either from the food or wine, but in any event, it was adorable.

"Help yourself," I said, swallowing another mouthful of

whiskey. "Have you ever traveled before?"

She took a piece of bread from the tray, and dropped it with a startled, "Oh!" She put her finger to her lips. "That was hotter than I expected."

I took her hand in mine and kissed the hurt away.

Her eyes widened but she didn't move to pull away. She sat stock still, watching me. I wanted to suck her fingers into my mouth and lick them, nip them, show her how dangerous I could be. But I had to keep myself tamed. Dropping her hand, I reached for the bread and tore it in half, waving it to cool it down before handing it to her.

"My sister called me," she said, her eyes cast down. She was confiding in me without being prompted. I schooled my face to keep it impassive as she spoke. Whatever that had happened may have upset her, and I had to keep my temper in check.

"Gavin, that — that..." She cleared her throat. "He wrote a story about my mother!" she said, her voice rising as her hands went up in protest. "Can you believe that jerk? He said that I'd tried to get her the help she needed but that you interfered with your big company, that you interfered by using your pull with local politicians, and that you'd made it impossible for me to have access to the medical resources that my mother needed."

I frowned, my appetite suddenly gone.

"Go on," I said.

"So my sister tried to intervene and call him out on the lies that he's spreading, but it turns out my *mother* was the one telling him all of this stuff to *begin* with!"

This was not good.

I chewed my bread methodically. "Very interesting."

She threw her bread onto her plate. "*Interesting*? I tell you that my mother has been spreading lies to the local reporter, who is now planning on doing an expose in the paper about you abusing your influence with local politicians and that's all you have to say?"

I shrugged. "Let him."

"And then he's going to prove that you have taken me against *my will!*" she said, throwing her hands up in the air.

Gavin could huff and puff, but he wasn't going to knock *my* house down. "Have another sip of your drink, sweetheart," I said, tearing another piece of bread, blowing on it to cool it, then handing it to her. "And have some more bread now that it's cool."

Sensibly, she obeyed, biting into the bread after dipping into olive oil, and chasing it with a long, thirsty sip from her wine glass.

"So Gavin's blustering nonsense about you being here, and has decided that he's on a witch hunt, and your mom is feeding his story. Anything else?"

"Nope that's it." She frowned, opened her mouth, then closed it again. Finally, she said, "Okay, so...you don't think this is a big deal?'

Shaking my head, I chuckled, though one of my hands was still clenched into a fist. I wanted to smack something — preferably Gavin — repeatedly, but it was more important that I calm her down.

"He's jealous of me, sweetheart, and loves that he can try to ridicule me for a story. Whatever. This isn't a big deal."

She looked visibly relieved, her eyes softening as she took another sip of wine. "Thank goodness."

The wait staff returned then with steaming platters.

"Oh. Lobster?" Annabelle said, eyeing the baked stuffed lobster. Our waiter placed the platter in front of her along with salad greens.

"Me, too," I told her. "I have my own trapping outfit on the other side of the cliff. We outsource the lobster to local vendors, who sell them fresh daily, but we have our pick whenever we choose. I have several different lines of business"

"Wow," she said, carefully removing a tender pink piece of lobster meat and eyeing it thoughtfully. "That's serious luxury, I'll tell ya."

I shrugged. I was a billionaire. Why wouldn't it be?

"Do you enjoy being wealthy, Mister — Sawyer?" she asked, as she carefully forked another piece of lobster.

"Yes." I sipped my bourbon and looked steadily at her. "I enjoy the lifestyle my wealth affords me," I explained. "I don't regret working hard so that I can reap the benefits of such hard work."

She nodded, taking a small piece of asparagus and nibbling it thoughtfully. "I see," she said. "Have you always been rich?"

I shrugged. "I've always been fairly well-to-do. You?" I knew she'd grown up poor, but I wanted her to confide in me. Not meeting my eyes, she helped herself to another piece of bread.

"I thought you knew my history," she said, her eyes shuttering as she looked at me. *Shit.*

"I do. But I'd rather hear it from you."

Her voice trembled a bit but only when she first began speaking. After a moment, her voice rang loud and clear. "I was from a family of average wealth until my father died," she said. "Then after he died, my mother took a really..." she paused, and sipped her wine again. "A bad turn, I guess you could say. She was in bed for weeks at a time. I was the only one who really did anything. I was fourteen at the time and my sister was twelve. We had no food, and our bills weren't getting paid. We had no family or friends who were willing to help. Things were getting desperate." She sighed. "So I took over. I contacted local people and got my mom on government assistance, but because I was the child contacting them, things went from bad to worse. They wanted to do investigations and things like that."

It seemed now that she'd started talking, she couldn't stop. Her wide eyes met mine as she sipped her glass again, and I realized it was empty. Without a word, I refilled it. "We were able to avoid any kind of interference from local authorities, and fortunately, my mom pulled through. She got out of bed and got a job, and we were...well, fine for a while. But she was never quite right after that. She lost one job after another until finally, after I graduated high school, I got a job of my own."

"You never went to college?" I queried. She'd graduated class valedictorian with perfect scores, and could have landed scholarships, no doubt. "You're very well spoken for a girl who never went to college."

"Thank you." She tore her bread harder than was necessary, and dabbed it in the olive oil. "I...I read a lot," she said. "One can make tremendous advances in one's education with a well-read mind."

I hid a smile behind my glass of bourbon.

She was so fucking adorable.

"So you went on to get a job in the local diner," I said. "Like George Bailey. Never got out of Bedford Falls, huh?"

Her cheeks flushed a bit as she sipped her wine, and when she replaced the glass on the table, she met my gaze. "I love that movie," she admitted, her voice a bit wistful. "I watch it over and over and over again. I *love* it."

I smiled and reached for her hand, squeezing it. "I'm not surprised."

"Well tonight, honey," I said, lifting a platter of stuffed mushrooms and offering them to her. "We'll travel beyond Bedford Falls."

She took a long sip from her wine glass before sliding it back on the plate. "Sawyer? I already have."

Chapter Twenty-One
ANNABELLE

Despite eating bite after bite of everything he offered me, the wine was going to my head. I knew it because the room swam a bit and his voice sounded a little distant, and when I turned my head to look at him, it felt as if it took several seconds to catch up. I blinked at him. He'd said something, but I didn't know what. "What was that?" I asked.

"I asked if you were ready for dessert," he said. Was it the wine, or the lighting, or my own altered mental state? He looked ridiculously handsome sitting across from me, his stern eyes matching the downward turn of his lips, a scowl that sent a shiver straight down the length of my spine as he spoke. His voice was so deep it made my nipples pebble at the sound. He was dressed impeccably in an expensive suit and tie, his dark hair falling across his forehead, lending him an air of mystique, danger, and intrigue.

I wanted him to take me. My panties dampened at the memory of the spanking he'd given me earlier that day, my ass still sore from the bites of the bath brush, and my pussy throbbed at the memory of his hand between my legs.

He was keeping himself at bay.

I needed to let the beast out. He would not hurt me. I was tired of him playing nicely.

"I am ready," I said. "I was starving, and the lobster was exquisite, but I can't wait to see what your staff does with dessert."

"I'm glad," he replied, but offered no further explanation. The wait staff came then, bearing trays of food that looked fit to be served to kings and queens. Puffs of golden pastry teeming with rich, creamy filling sat beside thick slices of layered chocolate cake, decorated with dark red raspberries and billows of whipped cream. Despite having eaten the appetizers and main course like I was a starving waif in a third world country, my stomach growled at the sight of the dessert.

"Holy...oh my...yum," I finished lamely.

He chuckled, then, a low, rumbling sound that made me shiver in delight. He didn't smile or laugh enough. It seemed I brought it out in him.

"Thank you," he said to his wait staff, taking the tray and placing it far out of my reach. What the hell? He waited until we were alone again in the room before taking an empty glass dessert dish from the center of the table and waving a fork at the desserts. "Are you a good girl, Annabelle?"

I swallowed, and licked my lips. I would play along. "Why, yes, sir, I am," I said, sitting up straight with my hands in my lap like good girls should. "May I...have dessert, please?"

"Please, *what?*" he asked, fork poised, his stern look skewering me in place.

I swallowed and pushed my thighs together. "Please, Daddy," I whispered.

With a nod, he pointed back to the desserts, and I realized he was asking which I preferred. "Chocolate, please," I whispered. He pushed it onto my plate and handed it to me.

"Enjoy, sweetheart," he said, getting to his feet. I blinked, startled. Where was he going? I didn't want him to leave. I needed him here with me.

"Why — where are you..." My voice trailed off, but he came to me and leaned over, kissing my cheek.

"I need to consult with Worthington on a few matters, Annabelle," he said. "Enjoy your dessert. In a little while, we'll leave for Paris."

I could barely contain my excitement, bouncing a bit in my seat as I sat on my hands to prevent them from clapping like a child.

"Should I go dressed as I am?" I asked.

He shook his head. "No, honey. Before we go, you'll dress in your pajamas, so you're comfortable. Okay?"

I smiled. "Yes, Daddy."

There were as many soft, plush pajamas in my drawer as there were dresses on the rack. Oh, God. This was amazing. As I pulled out a little pink pair of shorts with a tank top, I bit my lip, pushing aside the other clothes. I wondered if he'd put anything skimpy or skanky in there. I couldn't help but ponder what it would feel like wearing a luxurious silk teddy or a lace-topped babydoll. But no, there was nothing here but comfy, soft pajamas. They were neither old ladyish nor babyish, but rather classy and comfortable.

At home, I wore thrift store t-shirts and shorts to bed on warm nights, and I alternated two simple warmer pajamas for cold nights. I got by with a minimal wardrobe by washing clothes frequently and putting them out on the line to dry. It saved on electricity that way. I frowned, looking at the extravagant array in front of me. This was amazing, and I could have paid for my first year of college for the cost of this simple wardrobe alone. With that thought at the forefront of my mind, I chose the pale pink pair of shorts with a matching tank top, then slipped on a pair of flip-flops that were in the closet. I looked around for a bag to pack my things in, but no matter how hard I looked, none could be found.

"Missing something?"

I jumped. "Don't you ever knock?

"Door was open, Annabelle," he said, leaning casually against the doorframe. "And is that how you talk to me?" He raised a questioning brow and I shook my head, the responding thump of my heart in tune with the thrumming between my thighs. Damn, he had my number.

"I'm sorry," I said. "I was just looking through my things here...or, rather, I should say...these borrowed things here... and I'm a bit disturbed by how extravagant this all is."

He frowned a bit but didn't say a word. I went on. "And I'm not exactly sure how I'm supposed to...repay you," I finished lamely.

"We have an agreement, and I'll not ask more than what we've agreed upon." He looked almost hurt and angry at the same time. My cheeks flushed in shame.

"Mist— I mean, *Sawyer*, really, I...I didn't mean to imply that you're buying my favors or anything, I just don't know—"

"Annabelle, enough." His clipped tone arrested my speech. A beat passed between us, and then he took his hand out of his pocket, crooked a finger at me, and beckoned me to come to him. Dragging my feet across the plush carpet — wondering, wishing for, and dreading the possibility of a spanking — I went to him. When I stood a foot away, he leaned over, his massive frame taking up the doorway, needing to stoop just to reach my eye level. "I bought these things because I wanted to and because I could. I did not want you to feel uncomfortable. I merely meant to provide for a need a woman in your position has. Is that clear?" The gentle tip of his fingertip lifted my chin so that my eyes met his. My tummy flipped. His voice was soft yet firm when he spoke, his eyes earnest and wide as he gazed at me, his voice scolding. "What did I say about questioning me?"

I swallowed. "You said not to."

He nodded, his lips thinned, eyes still on me. "Are you questioning me now?"

I shook my head. "No, sir."

He nodded, satisfied. "Very good. Now come with me. We have a bit of time before our jet leaves after all, and there's something I need to show you."

Holding his hand, the feel of his rougher, warm hand completely engulfing mine welcome and tender, I followed him. We left the dining room and went down a hall I'd not seen before, a long hall that smelled faintly musty, as if no one had been here in decades.

"Where are we going?" I said, my voice just a whisper, as I felt the moment required reverence.

"Shhh, baby."

Down the hall we went, until I saw a faint yellow light ahead of me, spilling onto the thick carpet. An arched doorway awaited us, and his steps slowed. My neck prickled with curiosity, and I shivered. He pulled me closer as if to warm me. Faint strands of music wafted through the doorway.

"This was a very special place when I was a little boy. I was never allowed to go here unaccompanied, and only then on very special occasions. My father spared no expense, but it is so vast and opulent, I rarely go myself now. I had my staff prepare it for us, though, and now I'd like to show you to the ballroom."

I felt like a child on Christmas morning, eager with anticipation, excitement weaving through my limbs as he placed his hand on the small of my back, and with his other hand, pushed the door to the ballroom open. He led the way, and when I stepped into the room, I felt my jaw drop open.

"Ohhh," I breathed, as I spun slowly around, taking it all in as best I could. "Oh, this is magical," I whispered. The room was elaborately decorated in burgundy, gold, and blue, lit with glowing candelabras. In one corner stood a magnificent grand piano, gleaming obsidian black, the keys stark white below the glow of the lights. Music filtered in through hidden overhead speakers. Huge, oval paintings hung on the walls, and it was easy to imagine this magnificent place filled with guests, dancing in time to live music.

"You like it," he whispered.

"Daddy, I love it. I feel like a princess."

He grinned that rare grin that made his eyes crinkle around the edges, and his whole face light up. He extended a hand to me and I gratefully accepted it. "May I?"

I nodded, suddenly shy, as he swept me closer to him. "I...I don't know how to dance," I said.

"Just follow my lead."

And then we danced, and he was right...all I had to do was follow his lead. He took care of me. His steps were expert, his touch gentle but firm, and I was touched by the intimacy of being held by him like this, moved to near tears at the surreal moment that didn't seem to belong to *me,* Annabelle Symphony, the plain, poor schoolgirl who had nothing to her name.

It was *magical*.

We danced through two songs like that until finally, he pulled me to his chest and whispered in my ear. "It's time to go."

"So soon?" I sighed.

"I'll bring you back," he said. "I promise."

"But I haven't packed a bag —" I began.

He took my hand in his. "I had Millie pack your bag while

we ate. Grab your phone and your bag and whatever other girl shit you need, and let's go."

Stifling a giggle, my nerves raw and bubbly from the alcohol and his presence, I grabbed my things then joined him... on a private jet to *Paris*.

Chapter Twenty-Two

SAWYER

She sat next to me on the jet, looking tired but curious, her eyes wide and her mouth slightly parted.

"Do you just...jet around the country like this?" she asked, then, realizing what she'd said, she clapped a hand on her mouth as laughter bubbled up. She'd had more wine than I'd ever seen her have before.

Who knew she was a light weight?

She was an adorable drunk.

"Shh," I said. "Let's be quiet for a bit. We have a whole seven-hour flight ahead of us."

"Sleep?" she said, standing and looking out the window at the clouds below our window. "You want me to *sleep?* I'm standing in the middle of a bedroom in a jet in the air." She turned to look at me, and waved a hand at the large, king-sized bed next to the end table, and a small armchair. I'd had my jet outfitted for long flights, and I had no regrets. It was extravagant, yes, but it allowed me to sleep comfortably while airborne, and I fully planned on her getting her rest as well.

That was, until she decided to play her next move.

She sidled over to me and knocked against my knee. "Mister Gryffin?"

I growled. I was *Sawyer,* or *Daddy* to her, and occasionally *Sir.*

"I really want to kiss you," she said softly. "Up here, in the air, in this private bedroom jet thing which is the most amazing-freaking-thing I have ever seen *in my life."* We hit a patch of turbulence, and it didn't help that she'd been drinking. She wobbled on her feet and my hands instinctively encircled her waist, anchoring her to me.

"You're drunk, little girl," I began, regretting having allowed as much as wine as I had. I'd no idea it would affect her like this. "Honestly, you need some sleep, and I'm not going to --"

I would not, *could not* take advantage of her naiveté and innocence.

"Noooo," she moaned, her lower lip protruding as she pouted. It appeared she'd lost a bit of her reserve with all that wine. Fuck. How was I going to resist her? "I ... I really don't care," she said. "This is the stuff dreams are made of. I'll never have this again. I just want —"

Another bounce of turbulence hit and she flailed a bit. Holding her in my arms, I drew her belly-down over my lap. She squealed and her little hand shot back as if to block me, but I held fast, tugging down the sweet cotton pajama shorts and smacking her rounded ass before I could think this through.

"Enough talking back," I chided her, but when she wiggled her little ass at me, I lost my mind. I smacked her again, spanking with sharp swats that took her breath away. "You've talked back to me, told me no, and given me attitude since we left," I said. "I don't care if you're drunk. I know exactly how to sober you up." I spanked her until her ass was a bright cherry red.

"Okay!" She shouted, but that wasn't good enough. I smacked her again. "Okay, Daddy!"

I paused with my hand on her warmed ass and gently rubbed out the sting. "You are a naughty girl, talking back to Daddy," I said to her.

She swallowed and gulped, nodding her head. "Yes, Daddy. I'm so sorry!"

"Ahh," I said, my cock straining for release, pushing up against her belly. "Good girl."

She opened her legs then, just a slight part that made my mouth dry. She wore no panties, her pussy shaved bare, and her thighs glistened. I trailed my fingers along the hot edge of her skin, gently dipping downward, so gently that she shuddered at my touch. "Is that good, little girl?" I asked her. I wanted to lay her down on my bed so badly I could hardly see straight. "Is that what you want from Daddy, little one?"

I drew my fingers through her damp folds as she wiggled against me, eager for my touch.

"Come here, baby," I said, turning her around on my lap so that she faced me. "That's a very good girl for daddy." I cradled her in my arms. Tomorrow, she'd sober, and she'd feel the spanking even then. Would she remember what she'd done? I leaned down and took her mouth with mine, unable to stop myself from claiming the lips of the beautiful, infuriating women I'd just punished. Her back arched and her hands looped around my neck as she kissed me back, eager and receptive, our lips entwined in a lover's kiss.

I never should have kissed her. I could've kept my distance if I hadn't.

But now that I had, she was mine, and I needed her in every way possible.

Pulling her mouth off mine just long enough to whisper a plea, she begged me. "Take me, Sawyer. Right here on this bed."

"God," I groaned, my forehead falling to hers. "I can't. You're a virgin, baby. You're —"

"You've spanked me, kissed me, and made me come," she said, her eyes alight with passion. "And now I'm begging you. *Please.*"

"Is this the wine talking?" I whispered.

"Sawyer," she whispered back. "I was sober after the first spank."

Chuckling, I tossed her on the bed and stood over her, loosening my tie and watching her, all beauty and legs and curves, her tousled hair, her eyes tired but eager.

"You want Daddy to eat you out?" I rasped, wanting nothing more than to take her pussy with my tongue until she screamed my name.

She swallowed. "Oh God," she said, closing her eyes and licking her lips, her cheeks flushed bright pink. Her voice was husky when she managed to croak out, "I want it all."

I slipped out of my suit jacket and tossed it on a chair, then undid my shoes and lined them up against the wall. Next, I began to unbutton my shirt. Her eager, greedy eyes watched me, drinking me in.

I glanced at the door, hit the button that said *do not disturb*, and the lights dimmed. I'd set this up so I could sleep, and I was only to be disturbed under extreme circumstances. Given that I had a woman in the back of this jet — the *first* woman I'd ever taken on board — I assumed my staff would know better than to disturb me.

"You making sure no one comes in?" she asked, as she pushed herself up to sitting on the bed.

"Yeah, honey," I said.

Her eyes darted from side to side and her chest rose. She clutched the sheets in her hands.

I sat on the edge of the bed wearing nothing but my slacks, as her eyes roamed over my bare chest.

"You're amazing," she whispered.

I smiled at her. God, it felt so fucking good to smile at someone. How long had it been since I'd locked myself up in my proverbial tower, away from light and love and all things good? How long had it been since I'd *enjoyed* myself, actually looked forward to doing more than padding my bank account and closing a sale?

Too. Fucking. Long.

"Come here," I commanded, not recognizing my own husky voice in the small, quiet interior of the cabin.

Her eyes never left mine as she turned over and got on her hands and knees and crawled to me.

The sight of her on all fours coming across the bed to me made my cock harden, my stomach flip, and adrenaline surge through my veins. The vision of her tied up, hands over her head in helpless restraints, while I had my way with her flashed through my mind.

I'd have to remember that.

"Good girl," I said, reaching for her as soon as she was close enough to me, pulling her into my lap at the same time as I kissed her. "Never in my life has anyone told me I'm *amazing*. Why would you say such a thing?"

Her eyes closed momentarily before opening again, a quick glance at me before she looked away shyly. "So many things," she said. "I...at first, you frightened me. And honestly, Sawyer, you still sort of do. I mean, it's hot as hell being dominated by you, but it's also scary and I think..." She bit her lip. I reached to tuck a stray piece of hair behind her ear.

"Go on."

"I think that it's the scary part that *makes* it so hot. Not knowing exactly what will happen. Knowing you're the kind of guy who *could* hurt me..." Her voice trailed off, and her eyes dropped as she finished in a whisper, "But won't."

Never. I'd kill anyone who hurt her, and cut off my own hand before I ever allowed myself to do the same.

I'd spank her ass. I'd bring her to heights she'd never known. And I needed the control. I had to have it, like trees need sunlight or plants need water. But hurt her? Never.

"I wouldn't. Not ever."

"I know it," she whispered. "But it's more than that. You're...strong. And powerful. When I'm with you, I feel safe." She lightly touched the bandage on my side. "You rescued me. And I feel that there's an honesty about you I never really quite found anywhere else. I didn't even know I was looking for it. But there's no pretense, no pretending to be someone you're not. You can be an asshole, and you know it."

I raised a brow and she smiled, her lids half-lowered, giving her a fetching look. I slapped her ass, hard. She breathed in hard, and continued. "You're big. You're strong. And I feel like...I'm *yours.*"

My chest constricted. It had to be the wine talking. Where was the snark? The brat in her?

I leaned in and kissed the shell of her ear, then flicked my tongue out, carefully edging the soft, tender skin, the intimate feel of her warm body pressed up against mine making my heartbeat accelerate. "All mine," I whispered in her ear before I took her lobe between my teeth. I bit down lightly, then released it and continued to whisper. "All mine, and no one will come between us. Do you hear me, little girl? *No one.*"

I trailed kisses down her neck, loving the way her body rose to meet each kiss, how her head fell back in abandon when I got to her chest. I lifted the soft cotton edge of her night shirt, tossing it on the floor as I continued to kiss every inch of her curvy, voluptuous body. I laid her back on the bed and got to my knees in front of her, parting her legs and gently drawing down her shorts. I pressed my lips against the small slip of fabric at the apex of her thighs, and her hips rose as I teased her. Slowly, so slowly that she whimpered, I slipped a finger to push the edge of the panties over, and when I found her wet and wanting for me, I flicked my tongue along her clit. She grabbed onto my hair, her hips rising as I barely touched her, teasing, needing her to beg me before I gave in to what she wanted.

"What do you want?" I growled.

"Your mouth! *Please.*"

"Like this?" I asked, flicking my tongue harder against her clit, just enough to make her back arch again before I removed my mouth. "Or like this?" I sucked her clit into my mouth, and her hips writhed in response.

"Oh God," she begged. "Please don't stop."

I squeezed the hot cheeks of her ass between my hands as I took my time teasing her soft, feminine curves. She tasted so fucking good. She'd come hard after a spanking, I was sure of it. I released her right ass cheek and ran a hand up her side, pausing just long enough to tweak a nipple as I licked her pussy, until she writhed, coming hard against my mouth, so hard I had to hold her hips to anchor her. I wasted no time unbuckling my belt and swishing it through the loops. I doubled it in my hands, bent her over, and snapped the folded leather on her naked skin. She screamed out loud, then moaned, as I threw the belt to the floor, shoved my boxers down, and opened her up for me.

Leaning down to hold myself over her, I whispered in her ear. "Are you on the pill?"

She nodded.

"I want to take you now, Annabelle, and I want to do it bare. I want to feel your hot pussy gripping me when you come. I've been tested, and I haven't been with anyone this way in years."

She bit her lip. "Do it. Take me now."

I nodded. I was barely holding onto what little self control I had as it was. "Yeah, baby," I whispered. "I want you, too. Just let me know if I hurt you. I don't want to hurt you."

To my surprise, tears welled up in her eyes. She blinked through them and smiled. "See? You wouldn't hurt me, not ever."

I leaned in and kissed her tenderly, holding her sweet mouth in mine as I slowly, so slowly it hurt me, entered her. She gasped but did not cry out as I gently thrust in her, her tight pussy milking my cock better than anything I could've imagined.

I closed my eyes to the wonder of it all, wanting this moment to last forever, but needing more, needing friction. With careful, measured thrusts I built a rhythm. She was so tight, so perfect. I moved in her like we were meant to be together like this. My heartbeat raced as I claimed her, every thrust of my hips making her moan, her little fingers digging into my back until I couldn't hold out any longer and let myself go, the power of my climax overtaking me. I growled in her ear, needing to hold her tight, and she climaxed as well, shaking with pleasure as I rendered her helpless beneath me.

"Beautiful," I whispered. "So fucking beautiful."

Her eyes were closed but her cheeks wet. "Stunning," she finally said.

And as I held her in the darkness, I pushed away all the doubts that threatened to rob us of our joy. No, this would not last. It *could* not last. But I'd take what I could, and I'd take care of her for as long as she'd allow me.

Chapter Twenty-Three
ANNABELLE

I laid with my eyes closed in the darkness, sleep threatening to overcome me. I didn't want to sleep, though. I wanted to remember this moment. Where would I be a month from now? I never wanted to forget the feel of him beside me, his huge, hulking frame as gentle as a tamed lion, holding me against his chest as I faced him, snuggled up next to him, skin-to-skin. The prickles of his chest hair tickled my cheek. I clenched my thighs together, already the slight pain of him claiming me fading, as I reveled in the quiet stillness of my first-ever time making love.

How could I ever have imagined what it would have been like, being taken by him, his firm but gentle touch, his bridled strength making me wet for him before he even touched me? He was a full-grown man, bearer of terrible secrets, so filthy rich he wanted for nothing. Larger than life. He was arrogant and angry and had a temper that scared me, sometimes. But he could be sweet, and kind, and gentle. My big, beastly, gentle giant of a man.

"Are you tired?" he asked, before he reached for my hand

and brought my fingers to his lips. His warm mouth made me draw even closer to him.

"Very." My voice seemed as if it were a good distance away. I was so tired I could sleep for hours and hours.

"Then sleep, sweetheart. We arrive in Paris in four more hours. Rest while you can. Rest here with me, and I'll hold you."

My cheek against his big, broad chest, one knee hitched up on his, warm in the soft bed, lulled by the gentle hum of the engines, I fell asleep.

I woke with a start.

"It's alright, Annabelle," Sawyer's voice assured me. I blinked in the darkness of the dimly-lit cabin, trying to locate him. He sat in the armchair adjacent to the bed. He was bent over, tying his shoelaces. "We hit a bit of turbulence, but we'll be landing in about ten minutes. My pilot knows what he's doing, and we will be fine."

I sat up and pulled the sheets up to my shoulders. My head hurt a little, and it felt like it was stuffed with cotton. I closed my eyes and put a hand to my temple, massaging.

"Too much wine?" he asked. "You'll drink water and I'll get some food."

My stomach rolled with nausea, and I shook my head.

"No food?" he asked. I shook my head again.

His voice dropped, sterner now. "I knew that was too much wine for you. You're too young to drink that much."

I heard him get to his feet though my eyes were still shut tight, then the rustle of clothing moving approached me as he came to where I sat. I started at the feel of his hand on my neck, and his mouth came to my ear to whisper, "You've seen that I can be gentle, but I still expect you to do what I say.

And that, young lady, is non-negotiable. You had too much to drink, but I'll take care of you."

My fucking body *would* tense and heat at those words. I was thankful the sheet covered my nipples, which no doubt stood erect.

"Yes, Daddy."

God, I wanted him to take me again. My pussy pulsed, a responding clench low in my belly.

"Let's get you up and dressed," he said, releasing my neck and sadly, moving away from me. He reached for a bag in an overhead bin, and tossed it on the bed. I unzipped it, and pulled out a pair of jeans and a top, some panties, and a lace-edged bra, simple but clearly very well made. From another bag he handed me a pair of black ballet flats that looked both sturdy and adorable. Simple but nice.

"Dress," he said, snapping a tie in his hand and threading it across his neck. I blinked and looked up at him. He wore a white shirt, and a charcoal-gray suit that fit him to perfection. He looked freshly showered and ready to go. I fairly drooled.

"How did you do that?" I asked. He reached down to the bedside table and removed a bottle of water, twisted it open, and handed it to me.

"Drink," he ordered. "Do what?"

"Look like you're ready to hit Wall Street with the best of them. You look phenomenal."

He grinned, showing the whites of his teeth, before shrugging. "I slept like a baby, got cleaned up, and got dressed. Nothing to it, really."

"I probably look as if I slept in your back pocket."

His eyes twinkled at me. "I wish you slept in my back pocket."

I giggled, swinging my legs over the side of the bed and tossing the sheets aside. I stepped over to the bathroom and flicked the light switch outside the door. I shut the door, and heard him answer his phone, speaking in his typically clipped, business-as-usual tone of voice. I shivered.

I found a soft peach wash cloth, lathered it up, and quickly cleaned myself, brushed my teeth, and fixed my hair, dabbing on a bit of make-up just before I heard Sawyer calling my name from the other side of the door.

"Be right out," I said.

"You'd better," he told me. "We're pulling in for a landing now, and I want you out here, seated, and buckled."

So damned bossy and overprotective.

I rolled my eyes at my reflection in the mirror.

"Are you rolling your eyes at me?"

No fair! I scowled instead. "No."

"No frowning at me either, little girl. Now get your ass out here."

I swung open the door and stared at him, with a mixture of astonishment, irritation, and awe. "How did you do that? Do you have a camera in here or something?"

He smirked. "You're just predictable. You roll eyes, then scowl."

I began to roll my eyes but he held up a warning finger and shook his head.

At that moment, the plane lurched. I tried to grab onto something to steady myself but there was nothing but the smooth surface of the door. I went careening forward, but Sawyer was fast. He caught me, just before I slammed into the little end table in the cabin of the jet. He led me to a seat, leaned over, and buckled the belt for me. "Now sit, and be a good girl."

I did, feeling both miffed and turned on by his high handedness at the same time, just as a voice came over the speaker.

"We've begun our descent. We'll arrive in Paris momentarily."

I was thankful Sawyer sat next to me when we landed, because the jolt from the wheels touching down seriously freaked me out. I hadn't been on a plane before, and this was downright scary. I wondered if we were going to crash, but Sawyer assured me that we wouldn't. He held my hand, though, squeezing gently. I stared at his hands. His fingers were as large as sausages, his pinky easily the size of my thumb. Fine, dark hair covered the top of his hand, just enough to make him look masculine and a bit scary without being creepy. I could get used to this, this giant beast of a man holding my hand like this.

"You did a good job," he said, with an edge of pride. "People don't always like the landing. It doesn't bother me that much, but I get that it might bother others."

"It doesn't scare you? How is that possible?"

He shrugged. "I don't care what happens to me." He smiled as if he were joking, but something about his eyes told me he was not.

"Well, maybe *I* care about what happens to you," I said with a frown.

He smiled, then, though the smile didn't quite reach his eyes. "That would be nice."

He reached over and hit the button that said "Do not disturb" so the sign went dark, and a moment later, the door to the cockpit swung open and Worthington stepped into the room. I grimaced. If I had any idea it was Worthington in the cockpit with the pilot, I don't know if I'd have done what I did on that bed. God! I glanced guiltily back at the bed where the telltale tousled sheets told a story, my cheeks flushed with embarrassment, but neither Sawyer nor Worthington appeared to notice.

"Welcome to Paris," Worthington said with a smile. "It is precisely 4 a.m. here, and the business world is just beginning to wake. Our contacts in Asia are prepared for a 6 a.m.

conference call, Mister Gryffin. I'm assuming you'll be ready?"

"Of course," Sawyer responded, releasing my hand and rising. "Let's go, Annabelle."

I stood, and the little imp in me wanted to call him daddy, right here, where anyone could hear, but I bit my lip. Though a part of me wanted to be entertained by unsettling Worthington, I knew that Sawyer wouldn't approve. And all I needed was another trip over his knee. Hell, I didn't really like his disapproval anyway. It appeared he could read the little imp, though, as he leaned in and whispered to my ear, "Watch yourself, sweetheart. I can feel you ready to defy me even now."

I frowned, my head still hurting, and winced at the bright light when the overhead light came on.

"We'll get you something for that headache," he said, taking my bag out of my hand.

"I can take my—"

He silenced me with a look. Alrighty, then. It appeared I would *not* be carrying any bags.

The door to the jet opened, revealing a smooth, paved walkway.

"Local regulations make us land in the airport," he said, "though we don't have to do the same on our return trip."

Tired, my head still pounding, I allowed myself to be led to a waiting car. A driver opened the door, and I settled into the plush seat where we rode in silence for about ten minutes before we pulled down a narrow street.

"This is...this is amazing." I could hardly breathe. I forgot about my headache and the last twangs of nausea. This was unlike anything else I could've ever imagined. The sun was just rising in the distance, shades of pink and light blue mingling with the light, casting an ethereal glow over the most beautiful garden I'd ever laid eyes on as it passed our window. A brick wall surrounded what could only be described as an estate. The garden teemed with flowers, the trellis peppered with ivy.

"Oh, Daddy," I said, not even halting as the *daddy* tumbled out of my lips, "This is breathtaking. Where *are* we?"

"You like it?" he asked, his handsome face lighting up at my praise.

"Like it? I feel as if I've stepped out of reality and right into the pages of a fairy tale."

He smiled, his eyes twinkling. My tummy dipped. He was hot as hell when he was stern, or serious, but his smile was positively panty-melting.

"This is another one of my homes. I do business here a good portion of the year." I found myself reaching for him. I needed him to hold me. It was too much for me to take, sitting there beside him, drinking it all in. I needed to feel how real he was. He leaned in, his breath making the hairs on my neck stand on end. "Thank you for joining me, sweetheart."

I shivered in delight.

Chapter Twenty-Four
SAWYER

I always enjoyed Paris, but never as much as when I had Annabelle with me. I needed her to see how lovely it was here, to show her that there was more beyond the small, insulated town where she'd grown up. Here was an iconic place for her to enjoy, the most beautiful place that I felt was almost magical. Here, I'd make her mine.

"This is incredible," she said, walking around the garden, looking at the flowers and stone benches with an awestruck expression.

"Mister Gryffin, your first meeting begins in an hour," Worthington reminded me. I dismissed him with a wave of my hand.

"I know," I said. "But I need to take care of Annabelle."

"Oh, I'll be fine," she assured me, walking with wondrous eyes toward the entrance to my home. "I mean, surely something could occupy my time?" She looked at me, her eyes wide and expectant.

"Your headache is gone?" I asked with a quirked brow.

"Yes," she said. "Of course. I'm fine now!"

I smiled. It would be my pleasure to take her out to

dinner this evening, to treat her to the finest wines, to spoil her with pastries and fine food. Then I would take her back to my home...

"I know how you can occupy yourself," I said, doing my best to get my head back in the game, to stop thinking about laying her down and fucking her senseless, of taking her mouth with mine, or having her suck my cock. I would not be the beast to her. I would what she needed — her lover, her caretaker, the one who met her every need.

Her daddy.

I put my arm out to her and crooked my elbow, welcoming her to take it. Shyly, she did, her hand feeling so incredibly soft and fragile. "You said you like to read, didn't you?" I asked.

"Like?" she retorted with a laugh. "I spent my entire childhood reading, and have memorized every word of my favorite books." She smiled. "There is no frigate like a book..."

"To take us lands away," I supplied.

She beamed. "I didn't know you could do that. Emily Dickinson?"

I merely shrugged. "There are many things you don't know about me, sweetheart." I opened the door, and held it ajar for her, beckoning her to enter.

Several servants stood in the shadows, awaiting my instructions but prepared to stay silent and out of my way. In the large, airy entryway the floors gleamed, polished wood reflecting the overhead lights, and in front of us lay the majestic, sweeping staircase that led to the second floor. To the right lay my office, where I'd take my meetings today, and to the left lay one of my favorite places in the mansion — the library.

Releasing her arm, I stepped forward and pushed open the doors. The silver handles clicked open, the bottom of the door swishing over plush navy-blue carpet. I stepped in, taking in a deep breath, like I always did. I found the scent of books, mingled with the aroma of the wood on the shelves, peppered with the faintest aroma of the Cubans I favored, one of the most relaxing smells. I enjoyed a good cigar as I sat on the balcony and watched over the twinkling lights of Paris proper. There was something magical and otherworldly about it, and I loved having my own little secluded spot and not having to account to anyone in the small town to where I was chained. I loved my trips to Paris, but hadn't known how much more I would enjoy them with Annabelle by my side.

I stepped toward the humidor. I'd expected a fresh shipment of Cubans to arrive in time for my arrival, and as I was bent on seeing the newly-wrapped packages, I missed Annabelle's response to the room. When I turned to face her, her hands were up to her mouth. She spun around slowly, taking in the massive bookshelves I'd had built into the walls, filled to the brim with classics, fiction, non-fiction, anything I'd wanted and more. I'd kept my mother's small collection of paperbacks tucked away on one shelf. On another, I had every single work of Shakespeare and Chaucer, as well as some other famous British novelists I could not part with. I had a large collection of contemporary fiction but an even larger assortment of classics. She walked about the room on tiptoe, as if she were afraid of waking someone.

"You like it, Annabelle?" I asked.

Her eyes met mine in shock, as if she'd forgotten I was there. Spellbound, she walked over and pulled a hard copy of *Paradise Lost* from the shelf, allowing it to drop open in her hand, running her fingers along the smooth ivory interior as if she were smoothing away the wrinkles of a skirt.

"Like it?" she whispered. "I've never seen anything like it in my life."

Overcome with something I could not name, my heart constricting in my chest even as a dull sort of ache clenched in my belly, I swallowed hard against the emotions that threatened to overtake me. "I don't like it," she whispered. "Like is a paltry word that doesn't do justice to the magnificence of this room. I can't even...I don't even..." Her voice trailed off. "I do not like it," she repeated. "I am *madly in love* with this. I can imagine no other place in the entire world I'd rather be than right here, right now, surrounded by these books and..." Her breath hitched as she lowered her eyes shyly. "With you."

My throat tightened, and my nose tingled. She'd touched me in ways I could not quite fathom. She'd moved me, and my reaction had to be just right. She'd confessed to being happiest here, not only surrounded by her beloved books, but with *me*. The big, bad beast.

"You're welcome to come here any time you like," I said, my voice husky as I sought to control my emotions. "I know it won't be easy for you to travel to Paris, but you only have to say the word and I would make it happen. This room is yours, all of it, the books, everything in it. Well — everything except the cigars," I finished dryly, fairly certain that she'd not be too worried about that.

She laughed out loud, and it was the prettiest thing I'd ever heard.

"That's not very nice of you," she said with a coy look, her head tipped to the side, teasing me. "What if I happen to like cigars? What if I'd like to smoke one out on the balcony?"

She sauntered closer to me, her eyes fixed on mine, heated and challenging. When she was close enough to touch, I reached for her, pulling her to me firmly. "That's quite enough," I said. "Don't even joke about doing such a thing. I'd have to take you over my knee, you know."

Her eyes flared wider and her chest rose as she inhaled. "I know," she said. "Makes me want to light up right here and now."

I fisted my hand in the hair at the back of her neck, drawing her closer to me, when a sharp knock sounded on the door.

"Mister Gryffin?" Stifling a groan, I turned to see Worthington standing in the doorway, his brows arched curiously.

"Yes?"

"Your first meeting is in five minutes, sir. Would you prefer to take it in the library instead of the conference room?"

I released her, and stepped back. She cast her eyes down shyly.

"I'll take it in the conference room," I said. "I'd like to give Annabelle time to explore in here while I work. But when I'm done, I'd like our lunch brought out to the balcony, please."

Worthington nodded. "Certainly, sir."

"You're leaving?" she asked, after he'd departed.

"I need to," I told her reluctantly. "I have to take this call. I have a laptop set up with wifi in a little office on the balcony, and your phone should work here as well. Why don't you check on things at home? See how everyone's doing? We will return in the next few days, and it will be about that time that I am planning the interview about your being my wife. Sound good?"

She nodded. "Yes, Daddy," she said. "I would like that very much."

I pulled her to my chest, my cock tightening in my pants. God, would I ever get used to her calling me that? Would I ever feel that it was right? Would I ever get past the idea of scandalizing her, of taking advantage of her innocence and naivety?

She frowned, and her little hand came to rest on my cheek, her brows furrowed in concern as she looked at me.

"What is it?" she whispered. "Suddenly, that haunted look is back. The look you get when whatever eats you up inside has reared its ugly head again. Was it something I said?"

My hands clenched into fists at the very thought of her being at fault for what I'd done. I shook my head, one quick jerk. "Of course not."

"Something you're afraid of, then?" I wanted to ease that worry line between her brows, soothe it with the softest touch of my hand. I wanted to pull her up against my chest and hold her, and tell her there was nothing to fear.

But it would be a lie. There was plenty to fear, and the biggest of all was yours truly.

I could destroy her so easily. I could hurt her. I could *break* her. I did not want to. But I'd done it once before, and who was I to think that somehow I'd overcome who I once was? Who was I to think I was anything but the horrific beast the townspeople said I was? I had a whole room of letters and articles and evidence to prove it.

I let her go and turned away. "Make yourself at home," I said. "And I will join you for lunch as soon as my first meeting is over."

I felt her behind me. I could sense her hurt. I wanted to reach back and tell her I hadn't meant to be an asshole. I didn't mean to shut her off. We would make it right, the two of us, together.

But it would be a lie. I couldn't promise what I could not give her.

I never should have brought her to Paris.

Chapter Twenty-Five
ANNABELLE

Would I ever get used to the torrential mood swings of Sawyer Gryffin? Hot as blazes one minute, then cold as ice the next. My ass still stung from the spanking he'd given me, and my panties dampened at the mere memory. He was a man to be obeyed, a man who would never take no for an answer.

And God, was he a man. Nothing like the boys of my youth, and everything I could want. He ran deep, like the chasms of the Grand Canyon I'd visited just once in my youth, before my father passed away. I remembered what it was like standing on the precipices of something monumental and larger than life, knowing that what I could see with my naked eyes only barely scratched the surface of what lay deeper. And once I'd descended into the depths, I'd been held in rapt wonder at the majestic, fearsome, overwhelming beauty of it all.

Sawyer's passionate, broken, possessive, tortured self was beautiful to me. He needed a soft place, someone to come home to, a place where he could rest.

I wanted to be his soft place.

I wanted him to come home to *me*.

Deep down inside, I knew that if only I could get him to let me in, I could be what he needed to heal, the one he would trust.

I never knew what I was missing until I met him. A part of me even wished for a moment that I'd met him when he had no money, with no bargain or agreement standing between us, but I knew deep down in my heart that it wasn't his wealth that attracted me to him, but so much more. He was brilliant, and the depths of his passions ran deep. He was arrogant, I knew, and he was a man who liked to be in control

But hell if I wasn't a girl who liked to submit.

I wouldn't submit to just anyone, this I knew. I couldn't. I would never. But Sawyer? He unleashed in me forbidden desires I never knew were there. He made me feel alive, and special, and even now I longed to rush through the doors that separated us and reunite with him. He had his meetings in Paris later, but he'd return home and when he did... I'd run my hands along his back and neck, and watch the tension seep out of him. I'd listen to him when he had something to say, and offer my own perspective.

I wanted companionship. Passion. A real man, who could take on all of me and not crumple. I needed *him*.

I stared at the door for a good long while before I remembered that I was standing in the largest, most opulent, most exquisite library I'd ever seen in my life. I'd have all day to wonder about our relationship. Now I needed to get my hands on these books.

I pulled over a gleaming sliding ladder, and went up a few steps until I got to the very top. I just wanted to see what it was like up here. When I did, my head swam. It was crazier than I'd even imagined. The floor lay a good twelve feet below, and suddenly the ladder I held onto didn't seem so sturdy. I turned back to the bookshelves, and pulled one off, drawn to the emerald-green leather binding. *The Hobbit*.

Oh, no way. I flipped it open, the gilded-edged pages smooth beneath my fingers. Turning one page after another, I inhaled the fragrant scent of paper and ink, leather and bindings, the most calming smell of a library. Amazing.

I tucked that one under my arm, then chose a leather-bound copy of Shakespeare's sonnets, followed by a fetching hardcover version of *Madeline*. I would curl up on a chair and read about the little Parisian girl while sitting in Paris.

Paris! I'd almost forgotten we'd come all this way. I stepped down the ladder quickly, and walked out to the balcony. I sank into a cushioned chair with my books. Was this Sawyer's chair? I smiled softly to myself. I loved it.

The sun had risen a little while ago, and now was high in the sky, the warm rays beating down on me in my secluded corner up on the balcony. The comfortable chairs nestled next to a fireplace that was built straight into the wall, covered with an overhanging ceiling that I assumed would allow us to enjoy the cool evening air even during inclement weather. Office supplies were tucked away on a makeshift desk, pens and papers and a small, slim, silver laptop sat on top. They were all tucked so far into the desk area that the rain or sleet would never touch them.

An office in paradise. Astounding.

I put my feet up on the outdoor ottoman, and leaned back in my chair, propping up the copy of *Madeline* on my lap. I had just started when a buzz came at my elbow and a voice I didn't recognize came over a little speaker.

"Ms. Symphony, do you need anything at this time?"

Oh my. "I think I'm fine for now, thank you."

"A cup of coffee? Some food to tide you over, perhaps?"

A cup of coffee sounded delicious. And how often would someone bring me coffee and food while I sat on a balcony in Paris?

"Sure," I said. "A cup of coffee would be perfect, and maybe a little something to nibble on." I was feeling pretty hungry.

"Right away," came the voice, one I didn't recognize. Shortly after, I heard the door to the library open, and soft footsteps approaching me. Moment later, a young woman with her hair tucked into a little bun came over to me, a tray with coffee and pastries.

"Oh, this looks delicious," I said, extending my hand. "Annabelle Symphony."

The girl took it with a smile. "Maria," she said. "Pleased to meet you. Please do let me know if I can assist you in any way."

"Certainly. Thank you."

With a bow, she took her leave. I chose a flaky croissant and placed it on a plate next to a steaming cup of coffee. Then I simply savored the moment, enjoying the view of the garden below us while sipping my coffee, which was deliciously dark, laced with cream, just how I liked it. After a few sips, I placed the cup down and picked up my book, squealing to myself in delight. I was in *Paris*.

I leaned back in the chair, comfortably warmed and fed, and began to read but after a moment my eyes rested on the silver computer. I remembered with a start that I really needed to check in with my sister like Sawyer had suggested. She'd wonder where I was after a time. He said I'd have the ability to get onto my phone here. I picked it up, and took it out of my bag, powering it on. When I did, I blinked in surprise. Ten unread messages popped up on my screen.

I clicked on the ones from Melody.

Where are you??? I need you. There's an emergency with Mom.

I couldn't believe I'd taken off to Paris without telling Melody, without checking on my mom!

Annabelle? I need to talk with you!

Whatever you do, do not listen to what is on the news!

My stomach dropped, a cold chill making me shiver.

I dialed her number, and she picked up on the first ring.

"Annabelle! Oh, thank God. We were looking everywhere. Even Gavin tried texting and calling you. He sent a crew out to Gryffin's house to find you but you were both gone. Where are you?" Her voice was high-pitched and unnaturally tense.

"I'm in Paris." Guilt washed over me. I never should have come here. Who was I to think it was okay to come to *Paris?* Really?

She groaned. "God, Annabelle! Really? Paris?" Her voice shifted a bit with excitement. "Is it awesome?"

"I have no idea! I just got here. His home in Paris is awesome, I can assure you of that. But forget about that for the moment. Tell me what's going on!"

She sighed. "Well, you know Mom went to Gavin."

"Yes..." My fingers clasped my heart and I closed my eyes. I swallowed hard, willing myself to stay calm, an awful feeling of dread coming over me. "Then what?"

"Have you not been online?" she asked quietly. "Annabelle..."

Cold washed over me as I sat at the table, lifting the little laptop he'd said I could use and opening the lid. The second I opened it, the welcome screen flashed on. I clicked the button to take me online, and typed in *Whitby local news*. The front page of the Whitby Tribune came into view, the headline story with a picture of *me* no less.

No.

"Annabelle?" Melody's voice sounded distant. I shook my

head. This was...no...I couldn't even process what I was reading.

The police are in pursuit of none other than the infamous Sawyer Griffin, the man accused of being behind the mysterious death of an innocent female ten years prior, seems to have a penchant for young women. He's taken Annabelle Symphony into his home and now sources say they are traveling around the country together, against her will.

After the news of her kidnapping broke, Annabelle's mother was taken into custody for being a threat to herself and those around her. Mental illness is a strong suspect in this case. Local authorities are currently trying to track down Ms. Symphony.

I got to my feet.

"Annabelle?"

"They took Mom into custody," I whispered. "Where is she?"

Melody's voice wavered when she spoke. "She's at McGovern," she said, referencing the hospital outside of Whitby, the largest nearby hospital. "And they won't let me see her. They think somehow I'm not trustworthy since I had her here and Mom is telling them I wouldn't let her go. I don't know what to do, Annabelle."

"I know," I said, rubbing a hand across my eyes. "I will fix this, Melody. I promise, I will fix this. I need to come home."

"Will he let you? You've made an agreement to stay, and you'll make your agreement null and voice. Maybe he will not allow it!"

A strange sense of defensiveness came over me. "You don't know him," I said, needing her to listen to me.

She snorted. "And you do? You've known him less than a week, and now you're suddenly the expert?"

"It isn't like that."

"Yeah? Then what is it like? Want to tell me that?"

"Yes," I said through clenched teeth. "But not now. I will,

though." She would see, because now that I had him, I was not going to let him go. I was right where I was supposed to be.

Things would work out.

They had to.

Chapter Twenty-Six
SAWYER

I closed my laptop and shut off my phone, stretched back my arms over my head and yawned. When I traveled to Europe, I liked being disconnected, as much as I could anyway. Worthington made sure I wasn't constantly in the dark, and would feed me headlines as needed, but I mostly enjoyed the quiet.

I'd taken longer than I expected in my last meeting, but the deal was closed. Our clothing line would now be available to some of the most popular retailers in all of Europe. The expansion from American to European vendors was a huge one, and I was eager to celebrate, this time not alone with my cigars on the balcony, but with my girl.

A twinge of excitement tucked at my gut, a feeling I hadn't had in years, decades even. I had something to look forward to. Sighing, I glanced at the calendar on my desk. Only one more week until our agreement was up, and I'd fulfill my end of the bargain. But I'd taken such good care of her...maybe she wouldn't want to go home?

Was I fooling myself for thinking that she had any feelings for me? How could she? I was a beast of a man, an angry bastard who didn't take no for an answer. She hardly knew me.

There was a connection, though...

Or was that in my mind as well?

I pushed myself to standing,

I wanted her, here in my arms. I wanted to kiss her and hold her, and take her out to dinner under the twinkling lights of Paris. I would take her to my favorite restaurant, the little café owned by a married couple that did wonders with cheese and steak, we'd get a little table outside, and she'd order anything she wanted off the menu. I opened the door to my office, and I nearly yelled out loud as she crashed right into me, her pretty brown hair flying behind her, eyes wide and fearful.

What the hell had happened? Anyone who'd frightened her, scared her, hurt her, they'd answer to me.

"Sawyer! Oh my God. I need to go home." She slammed her hands on my chest, startling me. Was she in her right mind? "Now! Get your jet. I need to go!" She turned as if to run away, but I caught her.

She was such a fright I grabbed her arms and gave her a brisk shake.

"Annabelle," I said. "Calm down and tell me what's going on."

She shook her head from side to side. "I don't know. I don't really even know what's going on. I need to—you need to — It's my mom and Gavin and — I don't — help!"

Fear churned in my stomach but I had to master my emotions if I was going to help her.

"Honey, listen," I began. "I can't help you if you don't calm down and tell me what happened."

"Stop talking! Get the fucking jet!" she cried, pushing away from me. She was crazed, out of her mind. With one swift move I spun her around and cracked my hand across her ass. She gasped and jolted, but before she could respond, I swept her into my arms and held her in an iron grip.

"There's more where that came from if you don't calm the hell down. I'll spank some sense into you if you can't do it yourself. Understood?"

Her hands circled my neck and she rested her head on my chest. To my surprise, she closed her eyes as if she were ready to take a nap. "Yes," she said softly. "Yes, Daddy."

My heart warmed and my cock twitched. God, what this girl did to me.

"Tell me what's frightened you, sweetheart. We can't move any faster or more effectively by being frenzied. Explain what's happened, and I will do whatever it takes to take care of you."

She nodded against my chest, her soft hair grazing my chin, eyes still closed as I walked the length of the office, shifted her up a bit so I could open the door, then stopped into the hallway and marched purposefully back to the library. As I made my way to the entrance, she explained.

"My sister texted me, but I didn't get the messages until just a few minutes ago. I called her right away," she said. "It isn't true what they're telling people, Sawyer. I want to be here! I am not a prisoner!"

I nodded to placate her, the desperation in her voice making a lump rise in my throat. God, the poor girl.

"I know, baby," I said soothingly. "Now tell Daddy what happened."

Her shoulders relaxed as she leaned against me, her hands still around my neck. "My mother started telling people lies. They took her, Sawyer. They went right into my home and took her from us. She's being held at an institution, but they think she's crazy."

I shook my head. "You said she's unwell, but the visiting

nurses I've sent have said her illness is far more manageable than they expected. She isn't crazy, honey. We know that."

Her eyes welled with tears. "She isn't well."

"We'll take care of her. But now you have a big problem on your hands. You need to get her out of the institution and home again. You need to clarify to the media as best you can that you haven't been forced, and that you're here of your own accord."

"I need to go home, she whispered, her hand on my chest flat-palmed as if to show me how she was ready to submit to my answer.

"Yes," I said. "We'll go."

Even as I said the words I wanted to take them back, hold her close, tuck her into my arms and never let her go. If I let her go, would she come back to me? I closed my eyes briefly to help stem the swell of emotions that threatened to overtake me.

"But our agreement. It isn't *over*. I have another three weeks, and I haven't even had my big media debut yet. It's all in vain if I go now."

"That isn't important. Go."

"I...I don't know what to say."

I leaned in and kissed her soft cheek. "'Thank you, Daddy,' would do."

She clasped her hands about me once again, her gaze bright and hopeful once again as she smiled up at me. "Thank you, Daddy. I will come back. Sawyer, you have my word. I will come back."

But something inside me told me no, she wouldn't. She had no reason to.

I took my phone out of my pocket and powered it up. I'd send her home.

And then I'd find a way to live without her.

Chapter Twenty-Seven
ANNABELLE

He wanted to come with me, and God, I wanted him to, but as soon as we set things into motion for him to come, all hell broke loose.

"The authorities are looking for you," Worthington said, flicking through the news on his phone. "You're under no obligation to go back right now, and if you stay here we can at least get your legal team ready to defend you. It could delay things, at least."

Sawyer held his phone up to his ear. "I don't give a damn about any of that," he growled. "We will handle this when we get back to America. No. I'm not staying."

"Please, sir, listen to me," Worthington began, but Sawyer interrupted him.

"No!" he snapped. "You listen to me. I'm going with her. If they land me in jail until my legal team can bail me out, so be it. She does not travel without me. She does not travel alone. Am I clear?"

Worthington pursed his lips but finally nodded. "Yes, sir," he said, placing his phone back up to his ear. "Bring the jet. We leave within the hour."

"Sawyer, you do not need to go," I said, loudly so I'd be heard over the bustle around us. Worthington looked at me, and Sawyer's gaze burned a hole right through me.

"I didn't suggest it, or ask you. I'm going whether you want to or not."

I frowned, anger rising at his accusation. "I didn't say I don't want you to go," I said. "What I do not want is you bringing more trouble to yourself than necessary. I want to keep you safe here..."

"Enough, Annabelle."

"And if you decide you're going to..."

"I said *enough*." Damn. I'd almost forgotten how his dominating nature made my nipples harden and my panties dampen, even as I sought to control my anger at him.

"Fine."

He came to me, then, crossed right over to me and grasped my arm before leaning into my ear. "Try that again, or you'll be practicing that over my knee on the way home."

The vision of me sprawled over his lap, getting spanked on that enormous bed of his, as we traveled... "Yes," I whispered. "Yes, Daddy. I won't argue."

"Good girl," he said, pulling me into a ferocious embrace.

Tears pricked my eyes. I needed the fierce protection of someone who loved me, and he did. I knew he did. And I knew something else as well.

"I love you, Sawyer," I said to him. "I love you so very much."

His arms tightened so hard around me it almost hurt, but it wasn't tight enough. I needed to feel his enormous presence and strength now more than ever.

"And I love you, Annabelle."

Below the balcony in the garden, someone stirred. I wasn't exactly sure what or who it was, and I peered down below us, but they were gone now.

"Did you hear that?" I asked him, and he shook his head.

"Let's get you on that jet," he said. "We will sort this out."

---

*D*usk settled over Paris as the jet rose.

"Didn't even get you one full day here," he muttered, sitting back in the armchair with a glass of bourbon, frowning. He'd taken off his suit jacket and loosened his tie, and his hair hung over his forehead, disheveled but beautiful. I loved him so.

"After we get this mess settled, we can come back, maybe?" I asked hopefully.

He smiled, his eyes crinkling around the edges. He smiled so rarely that when he did it was a gift, something that moved me and made me want to climb on his lap and kiss him madly. "Yeah, baby," he murmured. "We'll come back."

My phone buzzed. Damn his international WiFi connection. I didn't get a break even when up in the air. Though a part of me was relieved to be able to see what was going on at home, every single update only aggravated me. I flicked through the messages and logged back onto Facebook, shaking my head in frustration as bullshit reports filtered my feed about my kidnapping and horrible mistreatment. I was told by his lawyer not to reply to anything in social media. Sawyer himself told me if I did, he'd spank my ass. I was being good but I was also checking every ten minutes.

"Annabelle."

I shook my head and waved a hand at him. "Just a minute. I am checking, still. There's a new article online. These bastards. If I ever get my hands —"

"*Annabelle.*"

He placed his glass down on the little table beside him, uncrossed his legs and opened his arms, the smile leaving his face and his voice lowering as he sobered. "Little girl, you come here."

I felt as if I walked to a lion in his lair as I approached, dragging my feet.

I realized then that he'd been calling me, trying to get my attention. His eyes never left mine until I made my way and stood between his knees.

"I called you, several times," he said, tapping a finger on my chin, and when I tried to look away, he grabbed the hair I'd twisted into a braid and pulled my gaze back to his. The sting of it tingled along my scalp, raising the hairs on my arms as my pulse spiked. I stared, and he stared back, and in his eyes I read so much more than I'd expected — sternness, passion, and an exquisite tenderness only someone close to him could ever discern.

"We have six and a half hours left of this flight home," he said. "When we arrive, the chances that I'll be taken into custody are high. I have no control over how things will go when we arrive home. Do you understand?"

I nodded, tears blinding my vision.

He released my hair, placed his hands on my lower back, and pulled me to him so that I sat on his knee. It felt nice sitting on his lap, where I was safe with his focus on me. He was so much bigger than I was that I felt wrapped in a cocoon when his arms came around me. I laid my head on his chest, and he held me tighter as he spoke.

"Do you like when I take care of you, Annabelle?" His harsh voice had softened. Though still deep, it was melodic and soothing, like a hymn.

"Yes. Yes, Daddy, I do," I said, enjoying calling him daddy where no one would hear, where I felt comforted and cared for. It was so wrong it was sexy, so taboo I trembled when I get up the nerve to call him that.

"I'm glad," he said in a low, deep voice. "But if you want me to protect you, Annabelle, you must do as I say."

Overcome with inexplicable emotion, I could only nod and swallow hard.

"Head on my chest like a good girl. There you go," he soothed. "Now, as I said, I'll likely be taken into custody. And it might take some time for my legal team to straighten things out. So, we have two choices. We can spend what could be our last night together for a while checking on the latest new articles online. *Or...*" His voice trailed off as his touch moved to the hem of my top, lifting it, exposing my bare belly that he tickled with the tips of his fingers. I shivered in delight and giggled. "We could spend the night doing far more pleasurable things."

I did not staunch the tears that flowed freely now, and allowed him to wipe them away with the pad of his thumb.

It could be our last night together.

"Let's do the more pleasurable things," I whispered.

He grinned, his stern features softening, his eyes alight with warmth and joy. His mouth dropped to my chest and he feathered kisses there, then trailed his tongue along the collarbone. I closed my eyes and let my limbs go boneless. He stood, lifting me with ease, and carried me to the bed, where he laid me down as gently as if I were made of spun glass. With gentle but firm tugs, he undressed me, baring me to him. He knelt by the bed and took my breast in his mouth, his warm tongue caressing my nipple so that I moaned out loud. I shoved my knees together, only to have him pry them apart with one hand while with the other, he kneaded my breast and flicked my nipple. He released me after a moment, and while I laid naked on the bed and he knelt in front of me fully clothed in an impeccable white shirt and dress slacks, I shivered with arousal. Slowly, he lowered his mouth between my legs, his tongue finding its way to my most sensitive parts, commanding control of my body. My body responded instinctively to his, already primed for climax. In a matter of minutes I came with abandon, his name on my lips, my body shuddering in pleasure as he held me in his firm yet tender grip, I could not think beyond what might happen, what could be, only content to be here with the man who loved me.

He climbed onto the bed and I watched in a haze as he stripped. He was so beautiful. And he was all mine.

"Sawyer," I whispered, gently training a finger along his large, muscled chest. "Mister Gryffin... *Daddy.*" At that, his eyes flared with heat and he lowered himself to me, nudging my legs apart.

"My good girl," he whispered. "Open for me, honey."

I opened my legs at the feel of his cock at my entrance, my heart skipping a beat as he thrust gently into me.

We made love until the wee hours of the morning, and when we finally collapsed on the bed in exhaustion, I snuggled up onto his chest, and we watched the sun rise over the Atlantic, a beautiful beginning to a day that would tear us apart.

Chapter Twenty-Eight

SAWYER

I wished I could have held her in my arms forever. I would have. I'd have neglected my own needs and given up all that I owned, every bit of it, if I could have only held onto her, protected her, shown anyone who threatened to tear us apart that she was *mine*.

I'd experienced terrible tragedy and pain in my life, but everything I'd gone through paled in comparison to what I faced now, letting the woman I loved go when I would have given anything to keep her.

We were almost home now, almost where we would land, and I wanted to be prepared for whatever would come my way. As per my instructions, Worthington had notified the local authorities that Annabelle and I'd be returning early this morning. I fully expected they'd be prepared to apprehend me, though the charges were false, of course.

A knock came at the door. We'd had "Do not disturb" on for the majority of the night, and now my crew was likely prepared to communicate. I sat up in bed and swung my legs over the side, before I leaned back and tucked the blanket around her. She watched me in silence.

"Come in."

Worthington opened the door and didn't even flinch when he saw her lying beneath a blanket on my bed. "Sir, we touch down in thirty minutes. Would either of you like something to eat or drink?"

"No, thank you," I said, looking at her but she just shook her head.

"No, I'm all set, too," she whispered. He nodded and left.

"Let's get you up and ready, then," I said. I lifted the blanket and leaned into her, pulling her over to me and cradling her on my lap. "Do you want me to dress you?"

She nodded. "Please." She closed her eyes as I laid her back on the bed and fetched her clothing. Her slightly-damp hair looked curly and unkempt and adorable. I helped her into a pair of jeans and a t-shirt, allowing my touch to roam the gorgeous curves of her body before I pulled the top down to cover her.

"There, sweetheart," I said, pulling her back onto my lap.

"This will work out, Sawyer. You will see. This is all going to work out."

I closed my eyes and nodded, kissing her forehead, and I held her in silence as long as I could, until we had to prepare for descent. When we were getting ready to land, I buckled her in and held her hand. Still, we said nothing as the wheels touched down.

I inhaled deeply as my staff prepared to escort us off the jet, and I clutched her hand as the door opened.

"No matter what happens, remember I love you," I said hoarsely.

His lower lip quivered. "I-I will, Daddy. I promise."

As I suspected, six armed men waited with weapons drawn when I exited.

I sighed. "Isn't this a bit of overkill?" I said, trying to be as nonchalant about all of this as possible.

The largest of them, still a good head shorter than I stood, stepped in front, his pistol drawn. "For a guy who murdered his fiancée and then kidnapped an innocent woman? I doubt it."

With a sigh I offered them my wrists. They cuffed me with more force than necessary, and tugged me over to the waiting cruiser.

Tears streamed down her cheeks. "I love you, Sawyer!" Her voice rang clear across the expanse between us. I smiled at her, noting the shocked looks on the guards who held me.

"And I love you."

"Stay strong. This will come right in the end!"

I did not reply. I could not give her false hope.

Chapter Twenty-Nine
ANNABELLE

Watching them take him away was the hardest thing I've ever had to do. I cried openly, not bothering to even attempt to hide my grief.

"It'll be okay," Worthington said, but I pushed him away, angry that he dared talk to me and attempted to console me. I wanted no one and nothing but Sawyer.

"Take me back to his house," I instructed the driver, but a policeman approached me.

"Ma'am, we were under the impression that you'd been kidnapped, and we'll have to bring you in for questioning."

"I'll do that when I'm good and ready. As you can see, I was not held against my will, I'm not hurt at all, and the only thing I want to do is to make sure my mother is okay."

I answered the briefest of questions from the police, as compliantly as possible as I knew that's what Sawyer would want. It seemed to take hours before they finally let me go and I arrived at his home. A sob caught in my throat at the sight of it, and I could hardly handle the emotions that threatened to consume me. It felt simply awful to be here without him. It was so wrong.

My phone buzzed and beeped.

Social media was out of control. Melody sent me article after article until I felt like I could throw up.

Psychopath strikes again
Kidnapping in our little town
Local waitress found.

I deleted them all and finally sent her a text telling her I was home, not to send me any more new articles, and where she could pick me up.

After asking the cab to wait for me, I raced inside the mansion and hurried upstairs to my room to gather my things. I stepped into the closet to grab my bag and books, tripping on something in front of me. Frowning, I picked it up. It looked like some sort of metal latch. I glanced up and my mouth dropped open in wonder when I saw the smallest little opening to an alcove. I saw where the latch had fallen off, maybe weakened with age, or perhaps it was meant to be, as I pushed the little alcove door open. It wasn't an alcove at all, but a little cubby space that I couldn't even fit my whole body into. Something cast a shadow on the wall of the little cubby. With trembling hands, I reached for it, coughing as a shower of dust came down on me. My fingers wrapped around the hard cover of a book. Curiously, aware of the time and importance for speed, I pulled the book down and let it fall open.

Written in large, loopy letters, lay the diary of Samantha McGovern.

~

"No, sir," I said, as my phone continued to beep and chime. Melody had taken me to the hospital to visit my mother, and now I answered questions from the local police department. It seemed the entire internet was on the attack against Sawyer, with Gavin at the lead. Post after post crucified Sawyer, making false, terrible accusations against him. His being arrested paled in comparison to the slandering that was tearing him asunder online. Gavin had riled up the masses, and the masses had predictably responded. "That is not what happened at all. All that happened was that I agreed to be his employee for a short time, to perform some tasks he needed."

My cheeks flushed at the memory of what we'd done together. I swallowed hard, and splayed a hand at my throat.

The officer questioning me just raised a brow and took more notes.

"And I believe your mother has been held for questioning as well, in the hopes that she will receive the medical attention she deserves?"

"This is why I've asked you to allow me to see her," I said between clenched teeth. "She needs regular psychological intervention, yes, of which I am aware and prepared to pursue, but she does *not* need, nor has she *ever* needed, to be committed to the McGovern mental hospital."

He held a placating hand up. "Fair enough," he said. "I'm merely doing my job here." He nodded. "She may go. Now take her to her mother."

Melody came to my side. "Oh, God, Annabelle," she said. "What a mess. Sawyer will never recover from the attack on him. They've made that clear that he won't. His career is ruined."

I shook my head. "He didn't take me against my will and you know it. I'll tell whoever will listen. If the attack is on social media, then it makes sense that the return defense will be on the very same platform." She took a right turn and accelerated as we got close to getting to where our mother was being held.

We finally arrived, and pled our case to the caseworker.

We were let in to see Mom, and she rose to her feet when she saw me. I embraced her, and she hugged me back.

"They found you!" she said. "Oh thank God, Annabelle."

"I wasn't lost," I said, my emotions rising as I whispered in her ear. "Mom, I'm fine. Really. I promise. Mister Gryffin is a good man, and he takes care of me."

"Okay," she whispered. "Then I was wrong to tell them you were taken? I woke up and was convinced you were. Did they come to get him? Will bad things happen now, because of me?"

I shook my head and swallowed hard. "*Wonderful* things have happened because of you," I said in return, my eyes filling with tears, and a sob threatening to choke me. I had to hold it together. "So very many things. But we need to get you out of here, and we need to prove your innocence!"

A deep, familiar voice sounded in the hallway. "...And just today, we've seen with our own eyes that Annabelle is no longer functioning at full capacity. Her presence with Sawyer Griffin has rendered her mentally useless."

Ha! What did they want to check? They could test anything they want and prove how Gavin falsified his news stories.

Gavin sauntered into the room. My fingers fisted and I wanted to punch his arrogant, handsome, foolish face for him.

I released mom. "What have you done?" I fumed. "You've set an all-out media attack on Sawyer! How dare you? He's done nothing at all to you. You ought to be ashamed!"

He signaled behind me, I assumed to his cameraman.

"Oh?" he asked, putting a microphone up to my mouth. "Tell us again, Annabelle. What he's done is foolish, is it?" He leaned in and whispered in my ear, "Agree to marry me, and this all goes away."

"Never!"

His eyes clouded and his jaw clenched as he spoke back into the microphone. "Our small-town waitress has lost her mind in the mayhem that surrounds her kidnapping, and it was only through the intervention of local authorities alerted by me that she stands here now, safe and sound, in front of us."

Anger roiled through me. "That is a lie," I said. "All a terrible lie." I took a step toward the camera. "This is recording? Then I have something to show you."

Gavin reached for me but someone pulled him away. I spoke rapidly, before I lost my spotlight, and I pulled the diary out of my bag. "The accusations against Sawyer Griffin are patently false. *All* of them. I went to live with Sawyer of my own accord, and he took very good care of me. In addition to his innocence as far as my kidnapping is concerned, I have further evidence that the murder accusations against him are also false!"

Gavin sputtered and writhed in my peripheral vision. I turned to look at him then, and gasped. It was not a security officer who held him, as I'd assumed, but Sawyer himself, no doubt released from custody and coming to get me.

He came for me.

His eyes fell to the diary as I continued as the cameras rolled. "This is a journal written by the very fiancée who you all believe was murdered in cold blood by Mister Griffin." I held it up. "Within these pages, written in her very own hand, is a vivid explanation as to how she planned to throw herself over the cliff to her death, how she'd planned it for months."

Pain flitted across Sawyer's features and his jaw clenched, but he held Gavin tightly.

I tapped the journal and turned to Gavin. "You want evidence and a story? Read this. But only if you rescind the accusations you've made."

He blustered and fumed, but he was no match against

Sawyer. "I will drop the story." Sawyer released him with a shove, and Gavin stumbled, reaching for the journal.

I looked at Sawyer, who nodded. He didn't want the journal any more than I did. It was a link to a past we would forget, the chains that bound him freed by the evidence I now held.

Gavin frowned at me but snatched the book, his eyes widening as he read the words.

Sawyer stood to the side, and opened his arms to me, his brows raised hopefully as he waited. Would I still go to him?

Cameras still rolling for all the world to see, I ran to him.

One month later

"Beauty finds Prince Charming," Sawyer read. He snickered at the headline of the article written for us, as I snuggled up against his chest in bed. "They're right about the beauty, but I'm no Prince Charming." He tossed the article to the side and leaned over to kiss me, his bare chest brushing up against mine. I'd thought our night of lovemaking had left me sated, but it turned out, I was wrong. I pressed my body up against him, needing to feel him all over again.

"Of course you're Prince Charming. What surprises me most is how they refer to me as *beauty*."

His hand cupped my jaw and I opened my eyes at the very moment he planted a kiss on my forehead. "There is no doubt about that, beautiful." I ignored him, ducked around his attempt of a kiss, and snagged the magazine with the article, reading loud.

"In a whirlwind of conflicting articles and erroneous information, the newlywed couple has made their debut. Mister Sawyer Gryffin, husband to Annabelle (Symphony) Gryffin, married his beloved wife, redeeming his reputation as a monster of a man. Whereas locals once thought him responsible for the death of his fiancée, they now tote him as "a benevolent benefactor," and "a true altruist. Ohh!" He'd snatched the article straight out of my hand and tossed it down.

"Altruist," he growled. "They don't know my wife is responsible for the attempt at vindicating my sordid reputation." He planted kisses down my neck and my eyes closed of their own accord. He was the master of my body, and I could do little to stop him once he started.

Not that I wanted to.

"No, they don't know that I was the one who orchestrated those donations, but they also don't know what a very good man my husband is."

His tongue flicked along my collarbone and then lower, as he worshipped my breasts, flicking his tongue along the sensitized nipple, drawing the tender skin between his teeth. He released me just long enough to hiss, "Fuck them." He pressed my wrists against the bed as he returned to my nipples. I sighed in delight. I loved him so much and it thrilled me to see that others were finally getting a glimpse at who he really was, a generous man who bowed to no one, who led with certainty... a man who loved me.

But my mind was growing hazy as he worked me over.

"No, Daddy. Fuck *me*."

"I love when you beg" he said, climbing on top. " I love you."

"And I love you," I breathed, as he held me close, in the arms of my very own beast, my friend, my lover. They could call me beauty, and I'd accept that I was beautiful to him. But the true beauty lay between us, the joining of two people who together, had finally found perfection.

EPILOGUE

"*T*his is the most beautiful thing I have ever seen," Annabelle whispered, staring out at the Seine, her little hand in mine. The diamond on her ring finger sparkled in the glow of the lights of Paris.

Mine.

She was mine, and would be forevermore.

Her mother had been released from the hospital a week prior, into the care of a full-time aide. She had a full suite in an attached apartment near my home. Annabelle would visit her as often as she liked. Her mother didn't like me at first, until I showed her her new home.

"You did this for me?" she asked.

"He did, because he cares about you, mom," Annabelle said. "Remember that what Gavin said about him was false. He loves me. We are going to get married."

And somehow then, it all clicked, and her mom had one of those rare moments of clarity.

"Oh, very good then," she said. "I do think it good you married into wealth. You know I don't have two pennies to pinch together."

We laughed at that, all of it, even Melody.

Annabelle took the money I'd insisted on giving her, the full payout I'd promised in our original agreement, and sent her sister on a European cruise. She'd meet us in Paris the following week, but until then, our time was our own. Annabelle no longer needed the money. She was mine now, my wife, and everything I owned was hers.

Gavin lost his job as reporter for the Tribune, and moved out west. Last we heard, he'd married the daughter of a wealthy Texas tycoon, and swore off the reporting industry. He now took small commercial acting jobs on the side, and managed his wife's money as a profession.

We kept our home on the cliffs, but hadn't yet come to a decision as to where we'd spend most of our time.

"Where should we stay?" I asked Annabelle, as she looked out at the Seine, sipping her glass of wine. She squeezed my hand in hers.

"Doesn't matter to me, really," she said with a shrug. "I don't mind where I am. I love all these places, because you are with me."

"I love you," I responded, bringing her fingers to my lips and kissing them.

She laid her head on my chest and squeezed. "And they both lived happily ever after."

THE END

A NOTE FROM THE AUTHOR

Thank you for reading *Beauty's Daddy: A Beauty and the Beast Adult Fairy Tale*. I'd love to hear what you thought about this book. Please consider leaving me a tip (otherwise known as a review) where you purchased this book!

Would you like to read a **FREE** bonus epilogue about Sawyer and Annabelle? Subscribe to my newsletter here: http://www.bit.ly/bdbonus

Thank you!
-Jane

ABOUT THE AUTHOR

Jane is a bestselling erotic romance author in multiple genres, including contemporary, historical, sci-fi, and fantasy. She pens stern but loving alpha heroes, feisty heroines, and emotion-driven happily ever afters. Jane is a hopeless romantic who loves the ocean, her houseful of children, her awesome husband, chocolate, coffee, and sexy romance.

You can find Jane at http://www.janeandmaisy.com

OTHER TITLES BY JANE YOU MAY ENJOY:

Contemporary fiction:

The Boston Doms:

My Dom

His Submissive

Her Protector

His Babygirl

His Lady

Her Hero

My Redemption

Standalone:

A Thousand Yesses

The Bound to You trilogy:

Begin Again

Come Back to Me

Complete Me

Western:

Her Outlaw Daddy

Claimed on the Frontier

Surrendered on the Frontier

Sci-Fi Romance:

Aldric

Idan

Anthologies:

Sunstrokes

Hero Undercover

Printed in Great Britain
by Amazon